THE ONE THAT GOT AWAY

DIANA RUBINO

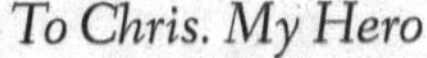

To Chris. My Hero

"We had a regular established line from Washington to the Potomac, and I being the only unmarried man on the route, I had most of the hard riding to do. I devised various ways to carry the dispatches—sometimes in the heels of my boots, sometimes between the planks of the buggy. Never in my life did I come across a more stupid set of detectives than those employed by the U.S. government. They seemed to have no idea whatever in how to search men."

— *JOHN SURRATT, DECEMBER 6, 1870, LECTURE AT ROCKVILLE, MARYLAND*

CHAPTER 1

Surrattsville, Maryland, April, 1854

"My children need a better life than this. Look at you—you're unfit to be a husband *or* a father!" Ma's wailing disrupted Johnny's sleep and jolted him wide awake. *Oh no, not another ruckus ending in Pa's stomping off and Ma sobbing.* He pulled the covers over his head.

"How can a helpless woman like me save their young minds—and souls?" Ma's plea reached Johnny's ears. He trembled, struck with panic. *My soul needs to be saved?* As those horrifying words echoed in his mind, Johnny slid out of bed and crept to the top step, pressing his forehead against the banister railings. If Ma couldn't save his soul, he needed someone who could.

"Some parishioners get a good Catholic education for their children, but they have their husbands' support, which I sorely lack," Ma groused, her back to Johnny. He pictured a bitter tear running down her cheek. Poor Ma wept a lot these days. His heart ached for her. He longed to comfort her but didn't dare go to her aid and endure Pa's wrath. "God bless my noble undertaking."

"Oh, give it up, woman!" Pa flung a cheroot to the floor and pounded it out. "There's good enough schools without Papist teachings."

"John, you are a blasphemer!" Ma sometimes used words Johnny—or Pa—didn't understand. "Worse than a misguided Protestant, you're a complete non-believer."

Pa flipped his hand as if to smack Ma. "You knew I wasn't a mackerel-snapper when we married. At least I let you baptize Isaac and Annah."

"Yes." Her voice lowered, defeated. "I am like the Eugenia of old. Her name epitomizes my own life. I would convert my family to the faith of the Holy Mother Church."

"Christ!" Pa kicked a chair. It crashed and splintered against the wall. "I even let you baptize my bastard son." Another family sore point that brought shame and ridicule upon the Surratts, especially in church, under nasty glares. Pa shouldn't have brought it up. Johnny's half-brother was named John William Harrison by his mother, Caroline Sanderson, who signed the legal papers "Caroline *Sarath*," in a misspelled attempt to lay the blame where it belonged. In response to Miss Sanderson's plea, the county court adjudged Pa responsible for the boy's upkeep.

"Fine wedding present *that* was, sir!" Ma's voice quivered, a sure sign she was about to weep. "Four months after our wedding, and me already in the family way with Isaac."

"Well, I done let you do it." Pa took a swig from his bottle.

"It wasn't *his* fault his father was irresponsible,"

Ma shot back. "I gave you my gracious acceptance of your affair. You are cruel, John, too cruel!"

"I, cruel?" Pa rasped. "And wha—wha'bout you?" He slurred his speech.

Johnny grimaced in disgust. *Once again, Pa's lushy.* "You oughta let well enough alone, Mary. You needs learn to leave things be. Hell's bells, you're in such a hurry to convert the world, you sold your own salvation by violating the Seventh Commandment. With a priest of all people!"

Ma raised and lowered her hands. "Shhh, not so loud, lest the children hear!"

But Johnny had already heard—although he didn't get the full meaning of "sold salvation"—and the Seventh Commandment? What was that?

"Bah! Little damned late for that, ain't it?" Pa's voice receded as he turned his back on her. "They heered it. It's rumored all over the county."

"Only because you cannot keep your inebriated trap shut!" They retreated to opposite corners, seething. Ma grabbed a bottle of Pa's and flung it into the fire. Glass exploded, shattering the silence.

"I would be well within my legal rights to shoot you without mercy, woman." Pa stomped across the room and halted before Ma. "No jury would convict me for your cuckolding. You ruined my family name and made me the joke of the county."

Johnny's heart took a sickening leap. No! Pa wouldn't shoot her! He silently vowed to bury every gun in the house first, knowing where Pa kept all three of them.

"If anything has ruined your name and made a fool of you in this county, it is not *my* action but *yours*. You are a perpetual sot, sir." Ma's slippers scuffed across the floor as she backed away. "Your whore is the bottle. You run up more debts each year. I try with all my might to keep this disgrace as much of a secret as I can, but your tawdry public displays of drunkenness, indebtedness, fornication..."

Fearing a physical exchange between his parents, Johnny perched at the top step, ready to burst into the parlor. Ma slid the pistol from its holster hanging from her chair. A cold puckering ran up Johnny's spine. But Pa held up his hands in a gesture of surrender. *Will she shoot him anyways?* Johnny swallowed a lump of fear and held his breath. To his relief, Ma held the gun out, butt first.

"Here! You go'head and kill me, John. It'll relieve me of the burden of being your wife and having to run this place. As for justifying my murder, try it and see how the courts treat you. You'll hang within the month. I will see you in hell, sir. In thirty days!"

Pa spat at her and stormed out. He slammed the door behind him, rattling the window panes.

Johnny turned and skulked off to bed, swiping at tears with his fist. Desperate to escape but needing to stay and protect her—he'd never felt so torn in his life.

He slipped back under the covers and whispered, "Where has it all gone so wrong, dear God? What made Pa such a poor businessman to run a saloon that's destroying the family? Is it my fault? If it is, what did I do to deserve the grief you've visited upon us? Why does he worship the bottle rather than Our Lord Jesus Christ?"

Oh, if only Pa could accept Christ, as he did. The call of the priesthood grew stronger every day.

~

Mary Surratt faced a dead end. Not even the arrival of Father Finotti's brother Gustavo from Italy took the edge off her worries about her children's future. But Gustavo married a local girl and established his own plantation a mile from the church, calling it "Italian Hill." Now Mary had new companions to help her pass the time.

In between visits to Gustavo and his new bride, a welcome diversion from her anxiety-fraught days, Mary dreaded the future and the completion of her new tavern home. She feared the establishment would attract an undesirable element—a danger to her children and a risk to the entire family's safety.

Sitting with Father Finotti at her scarred kitchen table, she poured tea into her grandma's delicate cups and placed a sprig of home-grown mint on his saucer.

"I don't know what's worse—when John is away in Virginia building the railroad, or home drinking." She released a forlorn sigh. "As for Annah, what kind of a place will a tavern be for a young lady to grow up in? I would like to send the boys to Boston College and Annah to Frederick, but I lack the money. Oh, Father, what can I do?"

"If you can't afford to send the boys to Boston and Annah to Frederick, then why not pick some local school?" Father Finotti sipped his tea. "You can apply for aid from the Church to reduce tuition."

"Right now I send the children to good schools, with no support from my husband—this is from a small inheritance from my father. When that's gone —" She couldn't bear to finish the thought. "I don't want to beg the Church. It's too humiliating. But I so wish a good education for my children. God forbid my boys should inherit any of John's sinful proclivities."

"What are the young'uns doing these days?" He chewed on the mint sprig.

"Isaac got himself a clerk's job in Baltimore. Annah's still at the Misses Martins' Female Academy, and Johnny wants to become a student for the priesthood. I'm thrilled at the prospect of him becoming a man of the cloth, away from the sins of the world, the constant temptations that goad young men. Most of all, history won't repeat itself. He won't follow in his father's debauched footsteps."

"They're on the right track, especially Johnny," Father Finotti assured her. "They'll become well educated and live better lives than we ever hoped to."

~

St. Charles of Borromeo College, Maryland, September 1859

John approached the meaty large-boned fellow and held out his hand. "How do you do? I'm John Surratt."

"Hello, John. Louis Weichmann." He took the outstretched hand and clasped it. "But I prefer you call me Lou."

Louis Weichmann's curly locks lay twisted in an oily glop on his head. His pince-nez glasses gave him a prematurely old, bookish appearance. His clothes, speech, and actions appeared so fastidious that it made John wonder—could he be a Nancy-boy?

Nah, just an insipid city boy lacking the rugged, outdoorsy feel of the men from Surrattsville. Older women tended to mother boys like him and let him escort their daughters. He could be trusted to keep his ideas—and his hands—to himself.

"I've so looked forward to making your acquaintance," Lou said. "We come recommended by the same man, Father Waldron."

John gave a one-shoulder shrug. "Well, my mother has connections, as they say."

"Yes, although my father is Protestant, my Catholic mother wants me to be a priest. I confess I have but little heart for it, but it's the best education our family could afford." Lou sounded sincere enough.

"I've wanted to study for the priesthood since I was seven years old. I prayed I'd be admitted to a school like this. I'm forever thankful God answered my prayers," John revealed, but wouldn't elaborate about his family or his abusive alcoholic father, one of his reasons for wanting to abandon the secular world and devote his soul to the Church. Lou didn't have to know all that.

"Actually, I was born in Baltimore, although I lived in Washington and Philadelphia," Lou told him. "In a sense, we're both Marylanders, I suppose."

John nodded. "Yep. Life here'll be rather restricted from the outside world. But sometimes that's what a man needs—time to meditate, to pray, and to find himself. I want to find out who I truly am. I figured the best way to do that was to enroll here, to see if this is my true calling." John glanced at the dining hall's austere surroundings, the three-legged stools and long planks set up as tables.

"Well, you won't be cloistered like a monk," Lou assured him. "We get Julys and Augusts for summer vacation. And each Thursday is our own, within reason. We have no studies then and usually go for lengthy walks through the countryside. But we don't get much time alone to *find ourselves*." He held up finger quotes. "We're escorted by the professors who wax prolific on various subjects, depending on what we encounter on the trails or sometimes by news of the day. And we're permitted to write to family and friends, without restriction."

"I got the impression from the fellas I met so far that most of the college is of a Northern bent," John ventured into touchy territory.

"Then *we* will have to defend the cause of the right, eh, John?" Lou placed a hand on John's shoulder in a hesitant gesture of friendship.

"You are indeed a son of Maryland, Lou!" John clapped the mild-mannered Lou on the back. He winced, but managed a hearty grin in return as he readjusted his specs, knocked loose on the bridge of his nose by the force of the blow.

John and Lou became fast friends, both orderly and studious, praiseworthy of conduct and deportment, although John liked to needle faculty by wearing a white necktie, rather than the usual black. During those supervised walks into the Howard County countryside on Thursdays, St. Charles's students came face to face with the real world. They learned about John Brown's Raid on Harper's Ferry, his subsequent trial and execution, and the election of Abraham Lincoln to the presidency. John didn't agree with the Republican president's principles. Seeing him as two-faced and power hungry from the start, he feared Lincoln would be the South's ruin.

One Thursday, deep in the Maryland woods,

headmaster Father Jenkins read Lincoln's first inaugural address to the hikers. "Any comments?" he asked. The "comments" evolved into a hot debate that divided the students on sectional lines. As Southerners, John and Lou stood for the Southern view. From then on, Father Jenkins kept the war as far from their minds as possible. But secession led to war preparations. As recruits practiced for war, the students witnessed the marching troops. The ear-piercing roar of musketry and cannon made Lou jump out of his skin, but didn't faze John. "This is just the beginning," he warned his friend.

The war came closer to home. John learned that his older brother, Isaac, had quit his clerk's job on the day of Lincoln's inaugural and left for Texas. He wrote to Ma that he had obtained a job as a mail rider on the line between Santa Fe and Matamoros. But he told John the truth: "I joined a Confederate mounted regiment of Partisan Rangers, one step above free-ranging guerrillas. Sure beats clerking indoors all year, but it's a long way from the impending Civil War." Whatever Isaac's reasons, John knew that the war had one good effect—it brought their feuding parents together as nothing had before. Both were avid sympathizers with the Confederate cause. John prayed for something positive to come out of all this destruction, division, and devastation, as he remembered his frantic childhood prayers. Now he begged the Lord for a Southern victory.

Back at St. Charles College, the war had its malicious effects, too. The more mischievous students began to sing patriotic songs—some for the Confederacy, some for the Union. The hikes into the fields and woods degenerated into mock battles between North and South. But the professors managed to keep the students from serious fights, restricting the struggles to competitive fun. It was an easy task—after all, the students were candidates for the priesthood, not seekers of military commissions and glory on the battlefield. Quarrels tended to the cerebral rather than the physical.

At the end of that term, John and Lou needed to decide their fate—either the cloistered life of the Church or back to civilian life. After much deliberation, long talks with his teachers and hours praying for the wisdom to make the right decision, John refused entrance to the priesthood. He went home to Surrattsville instead.

His family needed him more than the Church right now. Especially Ma, with Isaac gone. He would enter the priesthood after the war, not now.

"God bless you. You have been a good student here. We will always remember you," Father Jenkins bade John farewell.

But Lou resented the way they'd ignored his just-as-able scholarship. He'd wished to enter the theological seminary at St. Mary's in Baltimore, but they turned him down. Others, much less capable than he, got accepted.

Lou received an offer from St. Matthew's Institute in Washington City and took the position at once. It seemed a gold mine.

Lou hoped to meet up with John again soon. Quiet, shy, and with no confidence in social situations, he considered John the only friend he had in the world. John accepted him for who he was, approached him first, and offered his friendship. No one had ever done this before. He treated Lou with dignity, never calling him one of the many derogatory nicknames he'd had to bear through his life, like "Fatty", "Tubby", and "Blubberboy."

Yes, John was genuine, true blue. Lou now missed him with a longing that bordered on lovesickness. He desperately wanted John as a friend for life—and somehow, he knew their paths would cross again.

CHAPTER 2

Washington City, March 1863

As Lou trudged down the dark street between the school and his rooming house, a tall thin man accosted him. Fearing a robbery, Lou darted out of his path and prepared to bolt.

"Hello, Lou—is this any way to greet a friend?"

When he heard the familiar voice, he broke into laughter. "John!" He threw his arms around his old friend in a warm bear hug. "Oh, it's so good to see you again! I knew we'd meet someday soon, I—" He'd almost admitted he prayed nightly to be reunited with his only friend, but stopped himself short. "I sure have missed you, buddy." He stood back and looked John up and down. "You do look hale and hearty. Come on up to my room where it's warm and let's talk." He hoped he didn't sound too forward. But he didn't mind admitting—and in his heart he knew it—he wanted John all to himself.

"No, no. Let's go down the street." John steered him in the opposite direction. "There's a warm café open, and I'll buy us a coffee."

Lou fell into step with John and managed to keep up with his steady stride. They wouldn't be alone, but this was better than going another few years not seeing him, wondering how he was doing, unable to get in touch.

Seated across from each other at a cozy table for two, they ordered coffee. Lou studied his dear friend, drinking in every feature. His eyes raked over John's hair, the familiar shape of his head, his once-boyish features now more weathered, his eyes still wide with the innocence of youth, but wizened with the spark of maturity, his expression unusually keen and shrewd. His posture poised, his forehead still prominent, he was now more muscular. Back then, he'd been skinnier than a witch's broom. A wisp of a rust-colored beard under his lip made John look very much like a young Confederate President Jefferson Davis. John was now a man of the world rather than a student, bronzed from the out-of-doors. He exuded an air of self-confidence that Lou longed for.

"Life away from St. Charles College obviously agreed with you, John," Lou blurted out. Several patrons evidently noted the same to their table mates, as their arrival caused a stir. Sitting proudly with his friend, he wished with a tinge of envy it was *he* they were admiring.

The two chums quaffed their second demitasse by the time Lou finished describing his banal routine. "There's not much to tell about my dull life. So, what have you been doing, John?"

"I decided against entering the seminary. Since war broke out, I've devoted myself to The Cause. I promised Ma I wouldn't enlist, and if I get drafted, Ma promised I could purchase a substitute—if she couldn't scrape the money together, she'd sell the boarding house—so I'm doing everything else I can, and I daresay some of it's just as dangerous." He broke eye contact.

Lou leaned forward. "Dangerous how?"

"I couldn't sit back and let my homeland crumble beneath my feet, so I got involved, in a big way. Especially after the rail splitter got elected." A grimace distorted his features. "That was the straw that broke the donkey's back. So I've been riding the Confederate mails ever since I got home. We bring it up from the Potomac. Also send missives South from our agents in the North and Canada."

"How do you know which mail is for Richmond?" Lou struggled to keep the admiration in his tone—and the envy out.

"A cinch! It's all addressed to a fictional addressee, like 'Mr. C. Baker, Surrattsville, Maryland,' for example. There ain't no one by that name at Surrattsville, course. We grab all the letters for Baker and pull the covers off. Then we bind 'em into bundles and turn 'em over to a boatman at Chaptico, or Port Tobacco, or such places. He carries 'em across the Potomac and turns 'em over to another rider on the other side who takes 'em to Richmond. Things going North go in exact reverse," John continued, bubbling with enthusiasm. "Richmond gathers a bunch of letters and bands 'em all together. Then we run 'em across the Potomac. They get delivered to the nearest Confederate postmaster by fellas like me. There's lots of Rebel post stations in our area. The store in Bryantown, for instance, us, and plenty others. We strip the cover off each letter and stamp it with regular postage. Then Pa would send it on by regular mail, courtesy of the U.S. mail and Yankee tax money."

"*Would* send it on? What happened?" Lou itched to ask a string of probing, nosy questions. This venture fascinated him. He started to formulate a discreet inquiry about the Confederates needing extra help on these runs. It sounded a heap more exciting than the drudgery he plodded through every day.

"Oh, I got ahead of myself." John paused. "I returned home and started the mail riding. I no sooner got it well in hand—the Yankees are kinda dumb; they never search everything completely—when my Pa died in his sleep one night. I wasn't there." John's voice softened, eyes downcast. Lou detected a note of sorrow in his tone. He'd never mentioned his father, except in answer to Lou's quizzing about his family life—the tavern and the old man's drinking most of the profits. "He was never the same after he got kicked by a horse a couple years ago. Couldn't get around without the help of our slave, Dan."

"I remember at school you said he was pretty much the worse for drink," Lou offered a sympathetic tone.

John's brows knit, and he instantly looked years older. "Yeah. He got drunker all the time after the accident. Him and Ma fought like banshees over it. But when the war came on they declared a truce and turned their venom on the Yankees. They come down on Maryland with a vengeance, arresting members of the legislature and all. Some fella named Lafayette Baker." He took a breath, eyes now fixed on Lou. "Said he was a detective working out of Secretary of State Seward's office—later for Secretary of War Stanton. Guess they reckoned his methods were more suited to war than diplomacy. He flat tore Chaptico up. Forced the newspaper to print a so-called loyal edition, and deliver it to their subscribers." He chuckled. "Heck, him and some Yankee captain out of Fighting Joe Hooker's headquarters down at Rum Point—they arrested half the editors in the lower peninsula. Hooker is in charge of the whole Union army in the East now, you know."

Lou raised his chin with his own feeble attempt at arrogance. "Well, we *did* give them a scare when Baltimore rioted against the Federals coming through there to reinforce Washington. Remember how ol' Abe had to sneak through in disguise for his inaugural?"

"What a laugh!" John clapped his hands. "That lily liver hid himself in another train under a Scotch bonnet and cape and let his wife and boys face the brunt of the crowd."

Both men guffawed.

"My Uncle Zad was a real Union man at the beginning." John circled one finger around the rim of his cup. "Him and his friends actually raised Old Glory up the flag pole at Surrattsville and guarded it all night after First Manassas. But then he got to thinking about changing sides. It was when a punitive expedition from the 85th Pennsylvania Volunteers come down to arrest Rebels. They went after my neighbor, Ben Gwinn. They got him. A few others that were wanted lit out into Charles County and hid out at a doctor's house—Sam Mudd. The Bluebellies were so riled they couldn't find 'em that they wrecked the Gwinn place. When Ma gave 'em what for, they went over and burned our old mill on Oxon Run. Also rousted out some Italian who lived over there, an ol' boy named Finotti or something." His speech slowed as his tone intensified. "That *really* disturbed Ma. Ain't exactly sure why. She didn't care much about our mill, but that Italian's plantation..." He trailed off.

"Well, no telling when it comes to mothers," Lou offered.

"I reckon. My sister is the same way. She's all het up about Arthur Barry, a nice fella from around our neck of the woods, off with the Confederate army. She graduated from that Misses Martin's Academy. Now she pines away at home. Plays the melodeon real good—kinda like Ma used to do. Anyways, Uncle Zad didn't cotton to the arrests, property vandalizing, and the freeing of the slaves. That really ticked him off. Now that Pa's gone, he's a four-square Rebel. They used to argue all the time about the right of secession."

"Was your father ill?" Lou tried to sound casual, but he smoldered with curiosity about this intriguing clan. Why John never talked about them, he couldn't fathom. If he had a family this fetching, he'd never shut up about them.

"Yeah, apoplexy, I reckon. A courier from Alexandria come over to talk with Pa and Ma about the Confederate smuggling. Everything comes through our place—mail, goods, people, you name it. Anyhow, the conversation got pretty heated, everybody cussing the Yankees, Lincoln, cutting the right of *habeas corpus*, as they call it, that thing that gets you out of jail without charges being brought, don't 'cha know..."

Lou nodded in agreement. "*Everyone* in Maryland knows about the writ."

"...and freeing the slaves," John continued. "Reckon it proved too much excitement for ol' Pa. Ma woke up the next morning and there he lay, deader'n a doornail. Thinking Pa was paralyzed somehow, they sent for Doc Hoxton, but he couldn't get him up no how. I felt mighty poor about not being there." He paused with a faraway look in his eyes. "I was here in the city, selling vegetables. That's the way I hide delivering the mail. Why, we got spies all over the infernal Yankee government, even in Lincoln's own household. They all come down and buy from me and get their instructions and send whatever south to Richmond. Slick, I tell you!" John smirked with a smarmy haughtiness Lou never saw in him before. He now wondered—did John have a lady—or two—he paraded around town?

But Lou avoided that subject, knowing he'd stammer and stutter. Talking about the fairer sex, foreign territory to him, always made him queasy. Never with a woman in his life, he didn't know how to begin discussing the topic. So he stuck to family matters. "Ever hear from your brother?"

John nodded. "Yeah, we got a letter from Isaac last fall, still down in Texas and sometimes in Mexico. Says he's in some Texas cavalry unit, I don't know which. Some kind of Partisan Rangers."

"Sounds like a tough outfit," Lou remarked.

"I'll lay. Say, guess what. I work for the Federal government too!" John's voice lilted with pride as he sat up straight, threw back his shoulders and puffed out his chest.

Lou blinked in surprise. What else did the go-getting John have up his sleeve? He began to sweat, growing hotter with envy by the second. "A Reb like you?"

"Sure. They made me postmaster after Pa passed

on. Post Office at Surrattsville. Ain't that some punkins?" His lips spread in a self-satisfied grin.

"I reckon." Lou voiced indifference, but he truly admired his old friend. What a life in contrast to his anemic existence. He must ask John to give him a position somewhere. Restless, he squirmed like a child with his nose pressed up against a candy store window, his mouth watering for sweet treats he wanted so badly he could taste them.

"Your life sure beats school teaching night and day. If I had my druthers, I'd be happy doing half of what you do," Lou wangled his way in, seeking an angle. How to ask John what he really wanted? He tried, "You know, we need to see each other more often..."

John spread his fingers, palms up. "Why don't you come down home with me during Holy Week? I gotta help Ma figure out how we're gonna pay our bills. We had some hard knocks. Pa never paid nobody nothin', if he could help it. We fear losing the whole shebang, if'n we don't come through soon."

"That, my friend, is a deal!" Lou leaned forward and clasped John's hands. "I would love to see your home and meet your family!" *A great start!* He shivered in anticipation.

As he promised, John took Lou home to Surrattsville at the end of the month. Lou had never visited Maryland's lower peninsula. Due to rainstorms, the muddy roads and countryside looked bleak. Trees and plants still shivered in their bare winter coats. The low-hanging clouds kept the days gray and damp, hinting at more rain. Spring, still but a promise, eluded them.

Twelve miles below the City, Lou looked upon a clearing at a crossroads. As they traveled in a southerly direction, barns and outbuildings lined the road.

They finally approached a red two-story frame house. "Here it is, the old homestead," John announced. "I know it looks like something out of Hades itself," John admitted in an apologetic tone as their coach lumbered up to the carriage house door. "It's never been painted. Just another of Pa's unfinished projects."

"It's a palace compared to what I've been living in," Lou admitted.

"Ah, that's just a coat of lead primer." John regarded his family property with a furrowed brow and a frown. "Sorry it's not grander."

Wondering why John felt the need to apologize, Lou approached the tavern with a foreboding that Old Nick himself might appear at the door.

Instead, a black man removed the horses and carriage. "He's old Smithy, one of the former slaves," John explained. "Ma's now their sole employer." Under the short porch covering the entrance stood a stout dark-haired woman, beaming, arms outstretched. She hugged John, and he kissed her dutifully on the cheek.

"Ma, this is my school friend, Louis Weichmann."

"How *are* you, Mr. Weichmann?" She gave his hand a hearty shake. "I have heard so many fine things about you! Do come in out of the damp. Let's sit in the parlor and warm ourselves."

Unlike most people, Lou noted that Mrs. Surratt pronounced his name correctly at once. He wanted to thank her out loud, but was too self-conscious of his low, reedy voice to talk much.

Mrs. Surratt led the way into a hall that ran the full length of the house from front to back and motioned Lou to the right. A cheery fire crackled and popped in the parlor. Another servant took everyone's coats and carefully hung them in a closet under the stairs. *Mrs. Surratt sure has them well trained,* Lou marveled.

When a beautiful young woman appeared in the doorway and looked directly at him with dark penetrating eyes, Lou thought he'd begun dreaming. With a warm, but fragile smile, she stood tall like her mother, a much younger version of the matronly Mrs. Surratt.

"My daughter Annah. Darling, this is John's friend from the city, Mr. Louis Weichmann." Lou clasped the proffered hand, warm and soft. He nearly melted.

"How do you do, Mr. Wickman?" Her velvety voice enchanted him.

So besotted with her frail beauty, Lou did not notice the usual butchering of his name at first. Overwhelmed, he managed to stumble out an inane greeting. "Miss Surratt, I am honored. By the way, the name is Weichmann, with a long 'i.'"

"Oh, I am sorry. Please forgive my *faux pas*." She fluttered her hand over her lips.

"*Mais oui, mademoiselle.*" He gave a little bow.

"Oh, my," she giggled, "you speak French. And with a superb accent, too!"

"Not half as well as you do, Miss Surratt." His voice cracked as he pulled his collar away from his throat and gulped. His cheeks grew feverish. Sweat trickled beneath his underpants. Lou was not only burned with embarrassment, he was already desperately smitten. Oh, if only he could become a permanent member of this family he began to love as his own.

~

It didn't take Lou long to find out Annah and her mother were uncompromising Rebels and took every chance to demonstrate it—in ear-piercing, glass-rattling tones. At these moments they forgot they were nice Southern ladies.

"The damned Northern army and Abe Lincoln ought to be sent to hell!" Mrs. Surratt ranted on a regular basis with venomous hatred in her eyes, especially when speaking of Union victories in the West or along the southeastern Atlantic coast.

But Lou noticed that she never failed to provide a hearty meal and drink to any man or beast, Union or Confederate, who stopped by. He reckoned it was the matronly kindness instinctive of any sensitive woman, but his better judgment told him she covered her tracks well. He saw in Mrs. Surratt great force of character and a strong will.

Like the few older women he'd known, she showed the Old South style of hospitality, always feeding and fussing over everyone. She treated Lou like a member of the family, a third son. But she never referred to him in any manner except the formal "Mr. Weichmann." He, in return, always called her "Mrs. Surratt." But this bothered him. He'd hoped to take that next step toward acceptance as a surrogate son and call one another by their Christian names. He missed that closeness he'd never had with his own family. But he was happy enough just to be part of the household—and in the company of the lovely Annah, who captivated him to distraction. When her presence graced the room, he fumbled, tongue-tied, unable to find his voice. He didn't dare ask her to go for a stroll or sit across from her in the parlor over a cup of tea—alone. How much longer could he hide his ardor? She didn't go out of her way to be cordial with him. That made him all the more eager to win her over.

Lou met many of the neighbors at the tavern who came for their mail or a drink of whiskey or a segar or a chew of tobacco. He soon realized that the whole neighborhood was very friendly but out-and-out pro-Confederate in sympathy, just like the Surratts. Many had sons in Robert E. Lee's army, and others like John helped conceal Rebel agents and expedite the exchange of information, as did John. Indeed the whole route south that passed through Surrattsville was known locally as the "secret mail line." But it was hardly a secret.

~

The next morning, music and crashing cymbals jarred Lou awake. It blasted in through the window of the room where he slept.

"Hey, Lou!" John banged on his door. "Come on down! The Marines are here!"

He hurriedly dressed and thundered down the stairs. There in the yard stood a section of the United States Marine Band, the President's Own. "They're here to serenade some newly elected county officials,"

John explained. A frowsy-headed, sallow-faced youth with coal black hair acted very officious and overly friendly with the band members and everyone else. He seemed to be a kind of hail-fellow-well-met among the whole party. Seeing Lou standing next to John, the fellow brashly ambled over.

"And who is this rake?" he rasped in a tobacco-harshened voice.

"This is Louis Weichmann, my friend from St. Charles Academy. He's down for the Holy Week in a visit." He turned to face Lou. "Lou, this is Davy Herold."

"How do you do?" Lou extended his hand.

"Well, how do to you, too! I'm a graduate of Georgetown College, I am. Pharmacy. Sort of a fake junior doctor. That is, I make up and deliver pills that the sawbones prescribes. Got any ailments?" Herold grinned. "I'll lay I can find a pill to help get rid of 'em."

The band struck up a jaunty tune and formed ranks to march back to Washington. Much of the crowd followed, dropping off as they approached their farms or a side road home. Herold strutted in front of them, waving his arms in time to the music.

"I take it he's quite the Reb," Lou remarked to John.

"Yeah, a carefree type. He likes to hunt around, especially at Piscataway. Used to do it with his Pa, but he's dead. The old man was chief clerk at the Navy Yard. Herold knows the whole Marine Band. The members play at the various theaters when off duty and they get free passes they give away. It's a good deal. I 'low that Davy would get some for you, too, if'n you but ask."

The next day, Lou decided to take up John's suggestion that they take a couple of days to visit their old alma mater.

"Want to ride?" John asked.

"Oh, no!" Lou cringed, mortified at having to refuse. "A day in the saddle would kill me."

John didn't seem fazed. Lou expelled a relieved whoosh. He felt inadequate enough around his worldly friend—he needed learn to ride without John finding out.

"We'll just take the coach then."

At St. Charles College, the two former students renewed old acquaintances and enjoyed a whiskey with Father Denis. At the end of Good Friday, Lou turned to John and asked, "What's say we take a detour on the way back to Surrattsville to visit my old mentor, Father Mahoney at Little Texas. It's on our way."

"Did you say Little Texas?" Father Denis asked. "Here is an Italian newspaper, *Eco d'Italia*. Please take it and give it to a gentleman you will meet there, whom I taught at Montreal, named Henri Beaumont de Ste. Marie. You may use my name as an introduction."

When they arrived at Little Texas, John and Lou met Ste. Marie, quite affable despite his stuffy name. Lou took an immediate liking to him.

"I've had quite a time lately," Ste. Marie told them. "I'm from Canada, you know. I graduated college and went to work at a bank and then a store at Montreal. I was so attracted by your war that I came to the States to join the Confederate army." He paused for effect. "But I was caught or, rather, my ship was forced to heave to by a Yankee cruiser as we tried to elude the blockade. We all spent a horrible time as prisoners of the Federal government at Fort McHenry in Baltimore. I managed to convince them that I was but a harmless Canadian traveler and the British counsel got me let go."

"That's when you wound up here?" Lou perked up, curious about this man of the world, maybe even more sophisticated than his own John.

"No, I stayed in a flop house in Baltimore, and looked for a job to no avail. Then I became a day laborer on a farm. But I'm a city boy and quite unaccustomed to menial labor. One day this fine lady from Little Texas showed up, captivated by my good looks and gentlemanly manner." His lips tightened in a smug smirk. "She took pity upon me and secured me this job teaching at the Catholic school here. But I would like to do better."

"I know," Lou said, "I had this same job before you."

Everyone laughed at the coincidence, finding Ste. Marie's story humorous as well as interesting. That evening, Ste. Marie entertained them with his guitar playing and his fine tenor voice. An old Italian man arrived and sang some duets with Ste. Marie. They created exquisite harmony with their blend of tenor and baritone. It reminded Lou of the musical evenings at the Surratts', Annah's melodian playing and heavenly voice. With a warm feeling in his heart and a surge of excitement as he pictured Annah, he couldn't wait to get back there.

A few weeks later, Lou offered Ste. Marie an assistant teaching position in Washington. Once Ste. Marie was established in his job, he changed his mind, enlisted in the Union army and deserted to the South.

"I heard the Rebels didn't trust him and he became a prisoner of the Confederacy," John told Lou. "He barely escaped being hanged as a spy, saved only when he got wind of a counterfeiting ring and turned the perps over for his own hide's freedom. Course it's fairly easy to tell the difference between real and counterfeit Confederate notes," John explained. "The real ones have printing imperfections."

Oh, to be as well-informed and wise as John. Lou gazed wistfully at his friend. *Maybe someday...*

CHAPTER 3

"I NEED to check on some road information with Herold," John told Lou back in Washington. "You remember him? The erstwhile Marine Band leader? He's one of the sharpest guides around, knows the lower counties like the back of his hand. Better'n me, I lay, and I lived there all my life. I'm always looking for a new route to avoid Yankee cavalry patrols. If a body ever had a mind to pass through Southern Maryland, sight unseen, Herold would be the man to have at your side."

Lou heaved a wistful sigh. *What a romantic life, next to my own dreary existence.* Teaching day and night, not enough money to have fun on, everything geared to daily survival. It ate away at him like a canker. Seeing John so busy all the time, surrounded by intriguing people, with all this responsibility—he hungered to be a part of it.

He could no longer keep it bottled up inside. Beating around the bush and discreet hints hadn't registered with John. He blurted out in one breath: "Say, John, do you suppose I could do something to help

The Cause?" He wiped his sweaty palms on his trousers, leaving dark streaks.

Lou held his breath and counted an agonizing three seconds until John answered, "I'm not sure—you don't ride. Can you shoot?"

"No. But I can learn. You can teach me. I'm a real fast learner. Meanwhile, maybe I could get a job at Richmond." Now that it was out in the open, Lou no longer needed to hold anything back. "I hate my life as it is, John. The best weeks of my life have been the time I've spent with your family. I want to help The Cause. Please—give me something to do. I'll do any-thing." He knew he sounded desperate and pathetic. But now a strange relief calmed him, having spilled all. "I can't bear another day teaching boys their ABC's. I need to be a part of history, and John, you're my best friend—my only friend. You're the only person in the world who could grant me my wish." *Holy smokes, did I just say all that?* He cringed with mortification. But he dreaded the alternative—resuming his drudgery.

John's lips curled in mild amusement. "Well, I don't have many contacts below the river." He stroked his pointy beard with two fingers. "I tell you what. We need people here in the city. I'll keep you in mind, and if anything shows, I'll remember you first off. You sure you want to do this? It could get dangerous."

Lou's mouth dried up like cotton on a scorching day. "Oh—most—" He couldn't find his voice. His heart thudded. He trembled. Taking a long breath, he spoke: "Most definitely. Thank you, my brother." He grabbed John's hand between his two and pumped it with vigor. "You won't be sorry!"

~

During that summer, Yankee patrols came to Surrattsville almost every day, seeking to put an end to the smuggling of goods, messages, and folk from the ineffectual naval blockade on the Potomac. They stopped and searched the whole house for John, but found neither him nor anything else incriminating. But they were on to him, lacking only evidence for an arrest. During the last search, his mother played with Yankee frustrations, as she told Lou one evening over coffee and pecan pie.

"So I said to the Yankee officer, 'Now, I insist that you look in *here* for my son,' and I opened that closet under the stairwell on the second floor. And I said, 'If'n you do not, I must tell your commander that you did a poor job in searching this establishment!' And he high-tailed it out of here like a polecat after a warthog."

They shared a rare laugh. Lou knew she had a sense of humor hidden under all those skirts and rosary beads, and once in a while it peeked out and got everybody howling. Lou slapped the table with his palm as he guffawed, no longer shy around Mrs. Surratt. "Oh, Lordy Christmas, that's priceless! I wish I could send that to the newspaper."

"Maybe after the war, I'll put it in my memoirs." She gave him a sly smile.

"You're gonna write your memoirs, Mrs. Surratt?" Lou leaned forward with interest, knowing she wrote poetry; she'd taken some of her work out of hiding to show him, and he'd found it lyrical and moving. He'd nearly cried over the verse that proclaimed how brokenhearted she was at losing her true love. He didn't dare ask who this true love was, but reckoned it wasn't Mr. Surratt.

She shook her head. "No, who would want to read about me? I'll just fade into oblivion. I'll be happy if John becomes a war hero—that's good enough for me."

"By the bye, did the Yankees ever go poking around the hidden attic above the attached storeroom?" He knew it had windows to the outside that didn't show up inside the house. "Were they clever enough to find it?"

"Nothin' doin'." She shook her head. "I'd never say anything about *that* place."

"Good." Lou relaxed. John had shown him and sworn him to secrecy about anything having to do with the secret Confederate mail line—goods, people, and letters were stored in safety and secrecy.

John, whenever he was home, replaced his late father as the official Surrattsville postmaster. He enjoyed this job of Union postal clerk, his cover as a Confederate mailman, courier, and drug smuggler. Because of his growing network of connections, the tavern became a safe house where Confederate agents could rest up, hidden from prying eyes, on their way to and from Richmond.

John's job included such tasks as obtaining transportation for scouts and agents from the Potomac to Baltimore and Washington, and observing and reporting enemy movements on the Southern Maryland peninsula. He secured and forwarded Yankee newspapers, which reported Union troop movements and plans of attack and campaigns against Lee's Army of Northern Virginia. He forwarded books, small packages, Northern and Southern government communiqués.

Letters and messages were addressed in the normal manner, but lacked a return address and postage. They were bundled together and shipped across the Potomac. In Maryland, the Secret Line ran northward from Thomas Jones to Dr. Samuel Mudd, to John. At the Surrattsville post office, John broke open the bundles, affixed the proper postage and sent the letters on by regular U.S. mail.

The process southward to Richmond worked in exact reverse. All letters went to Surrattsville with one envelope inside the other. The inner cover bore the correct address for a destination inside the Confederacy. The outer one was addressed to Mr. C. Baker at Surrattsville, Prince George's County, Maryland. John would bundle the letters so addressed, minus the outer envelope, and send the bundle on its way in reverse, usually going through Chaptico on the Potomac, and by boat into Virginia.

Often the mail runner was none other than Surrattsville's postmaster himself. John made innumerable passages to the Potomac and at least a dozen trips across the river and on to Richmond. Crossing the Potomac was a serious matter, requiring the expert talents of boatmen like John's friend George Atzerodt. Travel north of the river was frequently by stage or rail. John made trips through New York and to Canada by way of the Hudson River Valley or even to Michigan and Ontario.

John became suspicious that Union agents were on to him. But he knew the Federal detectives seemed more interested in men who ferried quinine, morphine, and other drugs southward. They preferred to follow men like John to develop their contacts and routes of operation. John only wished he was the perfect spy, messenger, and drug runner—one who practiced deception successfully. But it was satisfying enough—and somewhat like spying. He only wished Lou would get off his back about wanting to join "The Cause" all the time. There was nothing he could give his friend to do, but didn't have the heart to tell him that.

In the fall, during the Maryland state elections, Federal authorities got a break that allowed them to move against John directly. After some snide remarks between pro-Union and pro-Confederate voters at Surrattsville, John's hot-headed sixteen-year-old cousin, John Jenkins, pulled a knife on one of the Union men.

"I will cut your goddamn heart out!" He slashed the weapon inches from Andrew Robey's face, son of the most outspoken Loyalist in Prince George's County. Lafayette Baker's First D.C. Cavalry, bivouacked nearby, came running up. Zaddock Jenkins grabbed the knife from his son and pushed him away. Then he turned it on the soldiers.

"You Bluebellies keep out of this," he roared. "I am watching these here polls and will be damned if I need any help from the likes of you or any other rotten sum'bitch who would vote for any damn rascal who would hold office under Abe Lincoln."

During their many tavern talks, John knew his Uncle Zad had changed his tune from when he supported the Union. He was angry at the Emancipation Proclamation. True, it had no legal effect in Maryland since it was a loyal state. It only applied to the states in rebellion. But Maryland was headed to emancipation of its slaves by state action, as bondsmen and women fled the fields for the freedom and safety of the growing Washington shanty towns. This was no time to risk being sold down south. The lack of labor threatened everyone's crops, and Uncle Zad was no antislavery man, not by a long shot.

As John feared, the angry Uncle Zad had crossed a forbidden line in criticizing the Lincoln Administration. The soldiers subdued him and he cooled his heels in the Old Capitol Prison for his lack of good judgment. Fortunately, he was on close personal terms with the warden, Colonel William Wood, and got sprung after the votes were counted. But the die had been cast, and ten days later John got fired as Surrattsville postmaster. His replacement was none other than Andrew Robey, who moved into the postal section of the tavern to keep an eye on the Surratts.

Robey's interfering eye was the last straw for John. His mere presence put a damper on the Surratt tavern as a Confederate way station at the heart of the Secret Line. So Mary took the opportunity to move her family into town. She had other reasons: the whole economy was shot to pieces, and the tavern was going broke. Her tenants vacated her Washington City townhouse, and John would be much better off with a position there. Most of all, she and her family were now trusted Confederate sympathizers, and her direct management of her boarding house would give the Rebel Secret Service a new secure base from which to operate.

When Mary and Annah moved to the city, Surrattsville performed a reduced role under its new tenant, John Lloyd. He settled in to running the tavern after the style of John Sr., including heavy imbibing of the liquid inventory.

Best of all, Surrattsville was now also shuck of Andrew Robey. As the only loyalist around for miles, his appointment as postmaster and ex-officio spy compromised John, long suspected by the Federals as a Rebel contact. With the Surratts gone, and no one to spy on, he moved the post office to his father's store down the road. No one was sorry to see him go. But the business brought in by postal patrons left with him.

~

Mary Surratt's narrow brick townhouse, purchased as part of a debt consolidation scheme of her late husband's, stood on H Street. The day they moved in, even before he assembled the beds, John hung the beautifully framed state seal of Virginia backed by two crossed Confederate battle flags with the inscriptions 'Virginia the Mighty' and Virginia's motto 'Sic Semper Tyrannis', *Thus It Will Ever Be With Tyrants.*

Mary missed Aunt Rachel Semus, her constant companion for the last six years, whom she'd left at the tavern to assist John Lloyd as cook. But her daughter Jinny moved into the boarding house to help out. "I feel much more comfortable having these folks close by. I'll always be a country girl at heart, and I'm ascared," she admitted to Annah. "I never dreamed I'd live in any city, much less the nation's capital."

When she read the *Observer* every day, her palms broke out into beads of sweat; the murders, the shootings, the burglaries, the poverty all terrorized her. Walking down the street was an ordeal; horse droppings covered the ground and raw sewage ran in a stream down the center of nearly every road. The stench of unwashed bodies jammed into the marketplace assaulted her. She wondered if she'd ever get used to it.

But she made the house into a home. She'd brought her favorite chairs and sofa, the melodeon, and her grandmother's silver and china from the tavern. She hung photos and etchings of popular war heroes on the walls and over the mantelpiece. The daguerreotypes were non-partisan: President Jefferson Davis, General Stonewall Jackson, General Beauregard, and Vice-President Alexander Stevens for the South. Facing them across the wall hung portraits of generals Fighting Joe Hooker, U.S. Grant, and George McClellan. Fittingly, the Southern portraits faced South, and the Northern ones faced North.

Mary's first and youngest boarder soon arrived. Honora Fitzpatrick, a plain girl with a pet cat, caused John to see her as bound for spinsterhood. Honora's father, a collector for several Washington City banks, told Mary he hoped that living with them would open up a new world for his shy daughter.

After the new year, ten-year-old Apollonia Dean, better known as Polly, also lived on the main floor. Mary hoped to secure three more boarders, to earn a bit of pocket change.

In mid-January, John made a suggestion. "Ma, I have a friend, name of George Atzerodt, who'd make a good boarder."

"What kind of a name is that?" She cast him a wary glare.

"German," he replied. "People up thisaway call him Port Tobacco—that's where he's from. You could call him that. He won't mind."

She wrinkled her nose. "Plug Tobacco? I hate the smell of tobacco."

"No, no, *Port* Tobacco. He don't smoke it, that's just where he's from. He's very important to the Secret Service. He needs a place to stay in the city. Why not rent a room to him?" he urged.

"He don't sound like a star boarder, or even a desirable one." She shook her head, sighing. "But I'm desperate. The cost of living here is dearer than I ever thought." She raised her hands, palms up. "Oh, well, why not? I'll let you act as my runner. I have to go down country for a day or so and take care of business. You may bring him in while I'm gone."

When Mary first set eyes on George Atzerodt a few days later, she recoiled as if struck. She'd expected someone like John or his college friend, Lou. But this man could hardly speak intelligible English. And he smelled—no, he flat *stank*—and looked seedy, like someone who lacked culture and any pretense of refinement. His rumpled threadbare clothes hung on his thin frame, his hair matted and greasy.

Within a few days, the maid came downstairs with the detritus from his room, an armload of whiskey bottles. Tavern keeper Mary knew that it was cheap rotgut not fit for swine. This was patently against the house rules. She was not about to abide another drunkard like her dead husband.

One night after the dishes were cleared and the others retired to the parlor, Mary told her son, "John,

I'm afraid your friend has got to go. I have soured on him, mighty quick. I will not have a man getting right smart for bark juice in my house every night."

John folded his napkin and placed it on the table. "But, Ma, he's very important. He's our boatman. Best blockade runner on the river."

"I don't care if he's Noah himself!" She ran her hands up and down her arms, chasing gooseflesh away. "He ought to swish his stinking feet in the Potomac next time he crosses. I allow that a few fish would keel over, if he did. We don't need such sticks around here. He gives me the willies!" She shuddered, clasping the pewter crucifix suspended from a chain around her neck.

"He ain't proper company for us women," agreed Annah, who'd come in to fetch the coffee pot.

John shot his sister a glare as if to say *you are not helping me one bit!* "He has no place to go, Ma," he insisted.

"I have no doubt of that." She cocked a brow. "I will lay that no one else will put up with him. He looks like a soaplock! I'll let him eat here on occasion and visit, if he must, but he cannot stay." She sliced through the air with her hand. "So help your poor Ma and get him out of here, at once. I don't need money *that* bad. Besides, I have a new set of boarders ready to move in. A whole family. Kin, too."

"He's flat broke, please, Ma..." John groveled.

She pulled five bills from her apron pocket and slapped them on the table. "Here is my last five dollars in greenbacks for your Mr. Plug Tobacco. I do not wish him to be thrown onto the streets without means. Let's hope he spends it on a hotel room and bathing water, not tar water. Now, clear him out!"

John respected his mother's wishes, and Atzerodt found other lodgings. His room in the front of the second floor went to the four-member Holohan family, distant cousins of Mary's. The bedroom to the rear was John's, when he was home. With its creaky bed, banged-up table from a rummage sale, rickety chair on its last legs, wardrobe, and two battered trunks, it fit his Ma's austere idea of "furnished."

CHAPTER 4

Lou, rebuffed at a second attempt to enter seminary in Baltimore, faced another dreary year of teaching at St. Matthews. When he learned of a clerkship at the Commissary General of Prisoners, a bureau of the War Department, paying twice what he currently earned, he pulled out all the stops. He secured letters of recommendation from Father White at St. Matthews and some of his fellow roomers, one of whom was an adjutant general with the Military District of Washington.

By mid-January, the new clerk was hard at work. With a spring in his step, he strode to the market place south of the capitol to share his good fortune with John. Afterwards, they strolled back to Lou's place of work, the War Department offices west of the White House.

Lou hesitated, for fear that John would question his motives. His breath caught in his throat. But he had to know. "By the way, John," he forced nonchalance into his voice. "How is your sister Annah?"

"Oh, fine." He flipped his hand in a casual wave.

"She was off visiting our Northern cousins in Ohio before Christmas."

Lou sought a way to ask how Annah felt about him, but John seemed not to notice. "Sorry I couldn't come down to Surrattsville for Christmas. But I felt obliged to go home."

"I understand. Ma was disappointed, of course. So tell me..." He slowed his step and cast a glance at Lou. "What exactly do you do at your new job?"

Lou's better judgment told him it wasn't such treacherous territory as discussing Annah. "Basically, I record statistics about prisoners of war—who is held where, how many, supplies needed, and such as that."

"By chance do you ever hear the passwords necessary to enter the city after curfew?" John pressed on.

"Not in my office." Lou shook his head. "But I think I know someone who might—a fellow roomer at my house. He's with the military headquarters of the city."

"Do you think you could get the password and countersign for...oh...let's say, tomorrow night?" John's eyes gleamed with intensity.

Lou pursed his lips. "At that short notice, I'm not sure. I'd do anything to help you, but I'm not that well connected."

"Remember how you wanted to help The Cause? I think we have a way you can." He cast Lou a cocky grin.

Lou halted in his tracks. "You mean getting the passwords and countersigns used at the bridges?" How exciting! And he'd be seeing more of John! His heart raced as he fought the impulse to reach over and give his dear friend an affectionate hug.

"Just the Navy Yard Bridge, the one that goes into Southern Maryland. The Confederacy needs military intelligence and you work in the midst of the biggest information factory the North has. We need your help. Think about it. Will it get you in trouble if I come up to your office and see you there?" They resumed walking.

Lou nodded, his breath quickening. "It will be all right at noon or after hours."

"Tomorrow noon, then? I will stand you to a lunch," John offered.

Lou tried to remember if he had any appointments. Then he said with certitude, "I'll be greatly honored to be your contact in the Union War Department. And I will have the password and countersign for the Navy Yard Bridge, or die trying!"

Since the war began, the War Department's woeful lack of security appalled Lou. If one could not find a specific bit of information in the blabbing newspapers, it floated down hallways, circulated round the urinals, lunchrooms, any hotel lobby or saloon.

John started coming into the office often, made friends with Lou's co-workers, and became so well liked, he visited whenever he felt like it. "Here, Lou, deliver this letter for me. It's been lying about in the U.S. government's bureaucracy for some time and needs some influence to hasten it along for proper consideration." He placed an envelope in Lou's hand. "It's an application for a government position," he explained, "now that we all live in town. I sent a copy to Congressman Calvert, but would you see that it gets into Secretary Stanton's office? Just to make sure it's acted upon."

"Glad to anything for you!" Lou clutched the letter, folded into thirds. After John left, he dashed to the urinals and tore it open.

Washington, D.C.
October 17, 1863

Hon. E. M. Stanton
    Secretary of War
    Sir;
    Having been informed that vacancies have lately arisen in the Paymaster General's Department...

Lou shook his head, baffled. *How did John know that? I never told him about it.*

...I have determined to make application to you in hopes of obtaining a position in said Bureau or in any other in which clerks are needed.

Though almost a complete stranger to you, I am firmly convinced that you will at least not cast aside my petition, especially when you reflect that I am the only son...Lou's eyes widened. *Whoa! He conveniently never mentioned his brother in the Confederate or Texas cavalry.*

...of a widow dependent, in great measure, on me for support. I have passed through a four year course of collegiate study, and my education is such as to enable me to fill any position to which you may think proper to assign me.

As to references, with regard to character or capacity, I most respectfully beg leave to call your attention to the testimonials by which this letter is accompanied... Lou nodded. *Oh, yes, they're all prominent Rebel neighbors in the Surrattsville area.*

Humbly awaiting your answer and confident
that you will do all in your power,
I remain Honored Sir,
Very Respectfully,

Your Obedient Servant,
J. H. Surratt

As Lou refolded the letter, he harbored a desperate
fear for his friend's safety, strangely mingled with another pang of envy. So John wanted to get in with the
"Lunatic Factory", as the Yankees called the War Department, with its numerous chances for spying. He
wished he had half of John's ambition.

~

Secretary of War Stanton had no intention of re-
plying to this letter. But he did have it copied and
turned over to his chief detective, Lafayette Baker, for
further use.

Baker, in turn, discovered John's dismissal from
the Post Office Department. It was not hard; he remembered the Surratts from his numerous visits into
Southern Maryland. Now he knew their contacts, including that fellow over in the Commissary General
of Prisons Office, who was he? Oh, yes...Louis Weichmann!

~

One evening when Lou was a dinner guest, he and Mrs. Surratt stayed at the table chatting after the others had removed to the parlor. He sensed something was bothering her, and felt he knew her well enough to ask. He certainly cared enough. "You seem a mite downcast, Mrs. Surratt," he ventured.

"Oh, nothing much." She sighed into her coffee cup. "Just the loss of a dear neighbor."

"Who is it?" he inquired further.

"The Finottis. Her parents have both passed away and there is nothing to keep them here. They're moving to Massachusetts to be with a brother."

"I'm sorry to hear that," Lou offered his sympathy. "Friends are hard to lose. I hope you'll be feeling better soon."

She looked up and straight at him. "I tell you what, Mr. Weichmann. How would you like to help? You could come and stay here, say, at thirty-five dollars a month, room and board. You won't find a better offer, and you'll be with your second family."

Tears of joy sprang to his eyes, and he blinked them away. "Mrs. Surratt, I am overwhelmed! I would be most happy to move in here at any price. It will certainly beat anything I can have in my current place. Thank you, thank you so very much!" He clasped her hands and grinned with relief, happiness, and the warm feeling of being wanted. Oh, how desperately he'd hoped to join their little household, but never dared ask, for fear of rejection. He could handle John telling him Annah wanted no part of him, but to be turned away from the door was more than he could bear. Once again, he had his family back!

~

On the happiest day of Lou's life, he brought his meager belongings through the Surratt boarding house door. As both roomer and boarder, he now had the best of all worlds—in warm, comfortable surroundings, rooming with John as he had in college, and taking his meals at a real family table.

Later that evening, he excused himself from the parlor and stepped up to his and John's room to dress for the local militia meeting of Company G, War Department Rifles. All government employees, especially those in the War Department, were obligated to join their proper militia company and engage in a weekly drill. Last summer, the Rebs had pulled off an attack on the city, so they needed be prepared.

Ideally, the militia was expected to help the Heavy Artillery hold the system of forts and rifle pits that surrounded the city until reinforcements from Grant's army could repel the attack. At least that's what Lou and his fellow enrollees hoped. More often they guarded government property at night. That was a mite more mundane to everyone but Lou, who loved strutting around in uniform. It made him feel like a real soldier. He kept it locked in the wardrobe so as not to upset the hand-wringing, rosary-praying Mrs. Surratt, worried sick that her John would be drafted.

Lou squared away the line between his collarless white shirt and his belt with the bright 'U.S.' buckle, and the fly of his trousers. Then he donned his wool infantry jacket and adjusted his kepi to a non-regulation, jaunty angle. He would pick up his outer belt, ammunition box, and backpack, rifle, and bayonet at the armory, but the men usually drilled without them. It kept the drunker ones from accidentally hurting themselves, a compatriot, or a civilian onlooker.

Checking his final appearance in the mirror, he gave his reflection a little salute. He quietly closed his room door and crept down the stairs, planning to exit the house through the servants' doorway in the basement.

Just about to sneak down to the basement, he halted in his tracks—face to face with Annah.

"Well, well, well. Looky here! A Bluebelly soldier ready to die for his country!" Her voice dripped with scorn. "Old Abe would be mighty proud of you, Billy Yank!"

His worst nightmare came true, finally being alone with Annah. He tripped over his tongue, seeking the right words to charm her. But even more agonizing, the most uncompromising Confederate sympathizer in the house had caught him in uniform.

"Come out, everyone!" she shouted into the parlor. "Come out! Come out! See the Bluebelly sneaking through our house. We've been occupied by the enemy and did not even suspect it!" Her shrill laughter cut Lou to the bone. A shiver ran up his spine. He quaked, unable to utter a word. He sweated as if thrust before a blazing fire, knowing his undignified squirming disgraced his uniform and the entire Union.

"P-p-please," he stuttered, "I-I have to attend drill...It's p-p-part of my job..."

By now Mrs. Holohan and Honora Fitzpatrick had joined them in the hallway. They snickered at Lou's discomfort and Annah's shrill laugh.

"I lay we can feel ever so safe, if the Rebs come!" Honora grinned, jabbing Mrs. Holohan in the ribs.

"Why, sure! We have our own *Yankee* parlor soldier to protect us," Mrs. Holohan agreed. "Chicken guts and all!" She reached out and flicked the gold braiding on his cuff. Lou cringed in shame as the two shyest and politest ladies in the house taunted him for doing his duty. He decided that the best defense was bold attack.

He cleared his throat and rustled up his voice: "You had better take care, you traitors, lest the real Yankees find out what hot-headed little Rebels you are. You will go to the Old Capitol Prison, certain!"

"You don't say," Annah huffed. Honora and Mrs. Holohan giggled, but Annah's scornful glare bit him to the bone.

Enraged, he clenched his fists, lowered his head and charged the ladies. They screamed and scattered to the corners of the room, but he pursued Annah.

"Lookit the little Yankee run!"

He grabbed Annah as she tried to duck under his outstretched arms. His arm closest to her got rightly around her waist but, as she struggled to escape his grasp, his other arm came around a little too high up her body, and he got a handful of her breast. His hand lingered a mite too long, and a thrill shot through him. Oh, how soft and delectable!

Annah slapped him sharply in the face. He regained his senses and released her. As she ducked away, she turned to face him, her eyes narrowed into hateful slits.

Lou was about to lose all sense of decorum when a new voice intervened.

"Stop it, all of you!" It was Mrs. Surratt, just come out into the hall. "Here I am, sick with fear that John will fall to the Yankee draft and all you can do is treat Mr. Weichmann in the most unlady-like manner!"

Mrs. Holohan clutched Honora's arm and they left the room, closing the parlor door behind them.

"Indeed, it would be just *too* bad to have two pairs of blue pants in this house!" Annah's words tore at him like claws. "I will lay that Mr. Weichmann is just about *all* we can stand without having anyone else dressed like a Yankee."

He gulped. "M—M—Mrs. Surratt, I—I am sorry. I tried to go out quietly..."

"Go on to your drill, Mr. Weichmann." She shooed him along. "Pay no heed to this."

"Yes'm." Tipping his hat to Mrs. Surratt, Lou stepped out on the front landing and closed the door to the street not too politely. He thundered down the outside stairs—no need to slip out secretly now.

"Sakes alive!" Mary turned on her daughter. "What do you mean, raw-hiding a member of our family thataway? And using the word 'pants' in public. I 'low as how this war has been the ruination of proper manners."

"What are you giving me Jesse for? He *touched* me, Ma, in a very rude and personal manner!" Annah shrieked.

"That's why young men and ladies ought not to cavort or roughhouse together." She shook her pointer finger in Annah's face. "It is up to *you*, as the lady, to set firm standards in how you treat a man, lest he suspicion your intentions."

"That's exactly what I *did*, when I slapped him!" She fixed her fists on her hips.

"Honestly, Annah! It should have never gone *that* far, and you were the instigator. Do it no more! Leave Mr. Weichmann be, Yankee uniform and all. He would never shoot a Reb, and he's too valuable a member in our own attempts to foil the Yanks and win this war to be put upon by you. Get along with him, *please*." She pressed her palms together as if in prayer.

"I will get along with him, Ma." She lowered her voice to a calm, conversational tone. "I will let him escort me to Mass, I will be civil in the parlor and the dining room. But I won't put up with his vulgar intentions, not for all the tea in China!" She turned on a heel and fled.

~

Outside on the street as he hurried to drill, Lou couldn't decide what hurt the most—Annah's smarting smack on his cheek or the pain in his heart from her hostile rejection of his harmless, boyish intentions. *Dear God, how I love her*, he confessed in silence, *Rebel sympathies and all!*

The next evening, he returned with an object wrapped up in brown paper—a picture of a pastoral scene labeled *Morning, Noon, and Night*.

"Do you think Annah would like it?" he asked Mrs. Surratt.

"Oh, yes!" Mary took the framed daguerreotype and held it up close so her myopic eyes could study the details. "Why do we not place it on the mantel and surprise her with it when she returns from the country?"

Several days later, when Annah returned, Lou showed her the picture he had placed on the mantel for her. She stared at it open-mouthed and slapped him firmly in the face. Stunned and humiliated, his lower lip trembling, he fled the room and dashed up the stairs. But the picture remained on the mantel.

He realized that, fond as he was of them, he would never understand the Surratt family. When his co-workers asked about the red marks on his face, he admitted that Annah had slapped him, but attributed it to a "political quarrel." He knew the clerks enjoyed hearing about his run-ins with Annah and her "Secession sympathies." Annah was quite outspoken in her sentiments, but John kept his political views to himself. Despite their intense conversations that ranged from ghosts to dinosaurs, they never discussed politics —or women.

"Whatever you do, don't tell Fatty," Annah warned Honora as she removed the picture of *Morning, Noon, and Night*.

"Oh, don't worry. I never talk to him anyway. He's such a Nancy-boy." Honora leaned over Annah's shoulder and watched her slide a small photo behind the one Lou had given her. "Let me take one more look, he's so dreamy!" Honora snatched the photo from Annah's hand and gazed upon it. Staring back at her with coal-black eyes, his curly black hair framing a marble forehead, was the handsomest man alive—the great actor John Wilkes Booth.

CHAPTER 5

"Your Ma's cookin'" sure hits the spot," Lou raved to John after dinner the night before Christmas Eve. "You Southerners know your vittles. Her corn dodgers are my favorite. My mouth waters every time I think about 'em." He followed John out to the porch so John could smoke an after-dinner segar. Mrs. Surratt forbade smoking in the house.

"Well, Aunt Rachel was Ma's cook for years, but since she's back at the tavern, Ma's been teaching her daughter Jinny how to cook. She's purty good at it, I do say so myself." John puffed on his segar.

"I never had garlic mashed potatoes before." Lou rubbed his hand in a circle over his belly. "My bread basket is stuffed; couldn't stop eatin' 'em."

"Yeah, just don't try to kiss nobody for the next three days." John smiled to himself, knowing Lou had never kissed a girl in his life, with or without garlic breath.

Lou looked out over the street and inhaled the crisp night air. "Everything seems so pristine, don't it, John? Been pretty nice for December."

John sniffed at the air. "Yeah, but somethin's

missin.' I know! It's the stench of that drainage canal that runs from the White House lawn to the Navy Yard." He screwed up his face, recalling the odoriferous combination of urine, human and animal feces, the offal of butcher shops, hotels, and households that floated through the city.

"Hey, John, some gents I work with think it right fittin' that the putrid canal runs from the White House to the Capitol. I heard others remark it's a shame that it runs in the wrong direction." Lou snickered. "Cynics, all of 'em."

"Yeah, and I ain't half the cynic," John agreed. "It's such a pleasant night. What's say we take advantage of the fresh air and walk down to the Avenue?"

"Great idea," Lou agreed. "I want to purchase a few Christmas presents for my sisters, and we can look in at the lobby of the National to see who's gracing our lovely city at Christmastime."

They went in and fetched their coats, scarves, gloves, and hats. "Ma," John called inside, "we're off for a walk down to the Avenue and back."

"Be careful, and don't be too late," came Mary's warning from the parlor.

They ambled down Seventh Street. "Ah, what a delightful evening." Lou inhaled the crisp night air. "The store windows look very gay." They turned and approached the elegant National Hotel. A gigantic gilt eagle perched on the porch roof, its wings spread wide in a welcoming gesture. Above the eagle a flagstaff hung suspended over the street, from which the Stars and Stripes billowed in the breeze. "Beautiful, ain't it?" John admired the scene. "A portrait of everything that's good in the North."

"Yeah." Lou nodded. "Let's hope this'll be the last full year of war, too."

They hopped onto the porch and John peered into the lobby. Several men sat around the raging blaze in the huge fireplace against the back wall. "Nobody important here, just the usual loungers and loafers. Now that I live in the city, I know the difference between loungers and loafers—loungers can afford to stay at the National, and loafers just sit here for style, before they retire to cheaper hotels and rooming houses."

"A perceptive observation." Lou glanced inside. "I'm not in the know like you, my friend. I don't know a lounger from a loafer any more than I know a bung hole from a hole in the ground."

"When I'm out late, I notice the downtrodden dregs of society cross the Avenue to Hooker's Division. Fighting Joe Hooker's headquarters were s'posedly among all the flop houses, gambling halls, saloons, and whorehouses that stretch between Ohio and Pennsylvania Avenues." He knew Lou wouldn't have set foot anywhere near there, he just wanted to titillate him a bit. "Course I steer clear of them places," he added, speaking the truth.

"Let's cover the whole square," Lou suggested. "We'll go along Pennsylvania Avenue to Seventh and walk back to the house that way."

As they passed the Odd Fellows Hall on the other side of Seventh Street, a voice came from behind them. "Surratt, Surratt!"

The two men stopped and turned. "Why, doctor, how do you do?" John called out to Mudd, standing with a strikingly handsome but shorter gentleman. "Let me make you acquainted with my friend Mr.

Weichmann, a school chum and boarder at my mother's house. Lou, this is Dr. Samuel Mudd, a neighbor from my days in the country."

"How do you do?" They shook hands. "And you, gentlemen, let me present you to my friend Mr. Booth. Booth, this gentleman is John Surratt. And his friend Louis Weichmann."

John had never met Booth in person, but saw him perform on stage. Up close he looked magnificent, rather than a blur from the cheap seats. A black mustache rendered the pallor of his countenance very noticeable. He possessed an abundance of black curly hair. His bearing was that of a man of the world and a gentleman. In dress, he was faultless.

John recalled that unforgettable line in a Washington newspaper article:

...and his eyes shown with an unwonted fire...

Now, up close, did they ever! Booth set those dark expressive eyes on each man in turn. "Pleased to meet you both." His voice was musical and rich in its tones. As he held out his hand and they shook, a thrill skittered up John's spine. The actor oozed charisma, onstage and off.

"We were just coming up to see you, John," Mudd said. "Mr. Booth wanted to meet you and discuss some matters concerning Charles and Prince George's counties with you. He seeks to know the roads to assist him in making some land deals."

"Please, gentlemen!" Booth flashed the perfect white teeth that made his smile the toast of the theater world. "Let's not discuss business on the streets like mere beggars. Why don't we all step down to my room at the National and ruminate over drinks and segars?"

"How civilized of you, old bean." John returned Booth's smile and they all set off two-by-two, Lou paired with Booth in the lead.

~

"Room eighty-four," Booth told the hotel desk clerk, "and send a boy up so we can order."

Upstairs Booth commanded the black porter, "Please bring up milk and rum punches and segars for four. And make it quick this time, Uncle," he added in a patronizing tone.

After the porter poured the drinks, Booth raised his glass in a toast. "Gentlemen, to your health!" They all echoed the sentiment and drank fully. Booth lit his segar and passed it around for the others to start theirs. The acrid smell of phosphorous filled the room as they sat smoking and relaxing. They exchanged small talk about the weather and the war without getting into more contentious issues.

"Where are you currently appearing?" John asked Booth.

"I'm taking a sabbatical." With a gleam in his eye, he added, "I've been concentrating my efforts in other areas." John figured he'd be telling them all about these "other areas" in a matter of minutes. From what he'd heard of Booth, he bragged endlessly about his exploits, his real estate deals, his business ventures. John didn't mind; he had nothing better to do.

During a lull in the conversation, Mudd asked, "John, might I see you outside a moment?" He addressed the others. "Won't you please excuse us, gentlemen?"

Mudd closed the door behind them. "Have you any idea why we're *really* here?"

"To hear Booth talk about himself?" John ventured with a facetious edge to his tone.

"No. And I must apologize for introducing you to a man about whom I know so little. But suffice to say that it's of great importance to the future of the Confederacy. We must keep what is said here in the utmost confidence." He kept his voice low.

John nodded. "I figgered as much. You'd better not include Lou, then. I ain't so sure about him sometimes."

"To be honest, I can't help but suspicion that Booth, himself, is a government agent." Mudd glanced over his shoulder. "But Tom Harbin confirmed all he said prior to today independently at Richmond."

"So let's go whole hog and hear Booth out," John suggested. "I'm eager to hear what he has to say." If he was a government agent, John knew his life was about to take an exciting turn. It wasn't every day a famous actor-turned-agent introduced himself and invited John into his inner circle. Goosebumps popped out over his arms and the back of his neck.

The two men re-entered the room to find Booth seated next to Lou reading aloud.

"That don't sound like Shakespeare," John joked.

Booth looked up from the sheaf of papers. "No, hardly. It's a government document a former congressional tenant left behind."

"Is it any wonder the South is doing so well?" Lou sucked on his segar. "It's hard to believe a governmental representative can be so careless with official documents."

"If they had any brains, they'd be in private enterprise instead of the government. Hence the low quality of our leaders," Booth cracked. John wished he'd said that.

"Say, Booth," Mudd interrupted, "would you step out with us a moment?"

Before Booth exited he turned to Lou. "Enjoy your segar, Mr. Weichmann, and have the rest of the milk punch from the pitcher. There isn't enough left for more than one. We'll return shortly."

As the door closed behind Booth, Lou decided he didn't like Booth any more than the overrated actor-cum-real-estate-speculator liked him. But then, Lou did not like *anyone* who monopolized John's time—that was, anyone who spent more time with John than he did. He'd admitted to himself at their reunion in the café, jealousy was one of his biggest downfalls. He wanted Annah, he wanted John—and he wanted them all to himself.

~

In the hallway, Booth turned to John. "What I am about to tell you is of the highest secrecy. You must give me your word of honor as a gentleman and a Confederate agent you will keep mum on this."

John shot Dr. Mudd a questioning glance. This was happening too fast to suit John's cautious sensibilities. The doctor closed his eyes and gave a reassuring nod.

"All right," John promised. "You have my solemn word."

"I have a proposition to submit to you, which I think if we can carry out will bring about a desired prisoner exchange between North and South." Booth's eyes twinkled.

John had been expecting something like this all along, but he still recoiled in surprise. He forced his eyes not to bug out with disbelief. "That's a gutsy move," fell out of his mouth before he could stop it. "Ferrying letters and messages is one thing, but an exchange of prisoners! That's something I never ventured to even suggest to somebody." He now had Booth pegged for a well-connected spy, not just some everyday government agent toady who carried out piddly tasks for his betters. If Booth was way up in the ranks, working with him would bring its share of rewards. He rubbed his hands together, eager to hear the details. "Well, sir, what is your proposition?" He hoped too much zeal hadn't crept into his businesslike tone.

"It is to kidnap President Lincoln and carry him off to Richmond," Booth stated as if announcing where they'd go for a hot toddy.

John gulped and nearly choked. "Holy smokes! Booth, what are you saying, are you cr—I mean, isn't that rather drastic? I hope you won't take my stance as a lack of respect or confidence in your abilities, but this is just too much!" John clapped his hand over his mouth; he knew he'd spoken too loudly. Mudd and Booth brought their pointer fingers to their lips. They listened for a moment, but the hall stayed quiet.

"Of course it's drastic. You might even say it's egotistical, megalomaniacal, illegal, and outright..." Booth flashed a grin. "Insane. But these are desperate times that call for desperate measures. I have it very well choreographed. This is no slipshod lark. The plan is to seize Lincoln, convey him by coach through Southern Maryland down the secret mail route, across the Potomac and the Rappahannock to Ashland Station, and thence by train to Richmond." He rattled off his plot with elaborate hand gestures. "All supplies and horses will be provided through me or other government representatives from Baltimore to Richmond. There he will be offered in exchange for all Confederate soldiers currently held in the North. What we need is more men. I understand you can help out in that matter." He leveled a stare at John.

"Doc," John turned to Mudd. "You say that Harbin is in on this? For sure?"

Mudd nodded. "Yes, he came in right away."

From inside the room, John heard Lou's chair scrape along the floorboards. Apparently, the others did, too.

"We'd better go back in. It won't do to have someone see us out here or for Weichmann to suspicion us," Booth stage-whispered. "I will call on you at your mother's place as needed—is that acceptable to you, John?"

Booth's use of John's Christian name made him feel like a real insider. The actor addressed the others with the formal "Mr. Weichmann" and "Dr. Mudd." But *he* was already the familiar "John"!

"Yes, so long as we don't include any boarders or my sister in it," John forced a stern tone.

"Done." Booth opened the door to room eighty-four and walked in. "How is that punch, Mr. Weichmann? And that segar? The hotel is renowned for both."

"Fit for a king." Lou had left his chair to lounge

on the fainting couch, his feet up. John wondered if that was all he had done. Besides basking in luxury "fit for a king," had Lou been listening at the door? What had he heard? John reckoned he'd find out later.

"Mr. Weichmann, my apologies for the private conversation," Dr. Mudd said. "Mr. Booth is looking to buy my land down state, and we were trying to agree on a price. I am afraid it was all for naught, I desire more than he will pay."

"Right. I had hoped that Mr. Surratt might be able to mediate, but our best efforts have failed," Booth concurred in such a convincing tone, John almost believed it.

The three men sat at the table in the center of the room, and Booth slid an envelope from his pocket. "I actually got lost on my way back to Washington the other day. Here is what I encountered. Perhaps, John, you might help me straighten it all out in my mind."

Booth drew a series of lines on the back of the envelope. John and Dr. Mudd leaned over the table to label and correct the lines Booth had made. Lou continued to peruse the government documents, glancing up now and then. John could see him trying to listen in on their conversation. He knew his friend was bursting to hear about the lines on the envelope. But the three kept their voices down and left Lou out. John realized how rude they were, but he'd apologize later.

Mudd stood and straightened his trousers. "Well, gentlemen, I'm already late for a prior appointment. I'm staying at the Pennsylvania House. Perhaps you'd like to walk with me?"

At Mudd's hotel, John saw that the subject of his

quest was already gone, so the foursome settled around the blazing hearth in the lobby. John held out his freezing hands and let the fire warm them as he flexed his fingers. Booth's room had been cold and the walk in the chilling air got him shivering.

Mudd sat next to Lou and kept him busy talking about the war. On the other side of the fire, Booth displayed a confident smile and reached into his coat pocket. "Permit me to show you my *bona fides*, John." Booth withdrew a pile of letters and handed them to John. The top one was his introduction to Charles County plantation owner William Queen from the now-deceased blockade runner, Captain Patrick Martin. John skimmed the Martin letter, glanced at the others from Richmond and Montreal, and returned them to Booth.

"Well, I've devoted my life as it is to assisting the South in gaining her independence, and I'll readily participate in any plan that might tend toward the accomplishment of that object," John stated with sincere conviction. "As long as it's honorable. The letter from Martin and the vouching of you by Mudd and Harbin are enough for me."

John silently schemed a moment and added, "We will need a boatman who can run the blockade on the Potomac. Harbin and I know one in Port Tobacco—George Atzerodt. We ought get Davy Herold, too. He's a local wing-shooter. No one knows Southern Maryland better than him—not even me. You already have some men of your own, I assume?"

Booth nodded. "I have a couple of ex-Confederate soldiers out of Baltimore. I'm working on a few of my actor friends. And I know Herold, too, from the theater—a hanger-on, but he's a chief cook and bottle washer of sorts."

"I decided to forego the priesthood to devote my life to The Cause and readily accept assignments that take me as far afield as Canada." John made sure Booth knew he'd be an essential participant in his campaign—knowledgeable, loyal to the South, and daring.

Booth showed him some more letters, but these were of a much more intimate nature—missives of unrequited love from ladies, signatures scratched over or cut out entirely. John marveled over all of them, especially the gushings about Booth's prowess as a womanizer. A twinge of envy niggled at him, but after all, Booth had five years on him. John had some catching up to do, but plenty of time to do it.

About 10:30, Booth excused himself for the night. Outside, John and Lou bundled themselves against the cold and strode at a brisk pace. John pictured his mother rocking in her chair, hands clasped around her rosary beads, chanting Hail Marys for their safe return.

"Did you know that the man you met this evening was the famous thespian, the tragedian John Wilkes Booth, from the family of the same name?" John asked.

"Booth? The land buyer?" He tossed his head. "I've seen him on the stage." He hardly sounded impressed. "But he can't hold a candle to his brothers. I didn't even recognize Booth at first. I thought Dr. Mudd had called him Boone!"

Lou was as outwardly envious as John expected. But he knew the always-snooping Lou had listened at the door after hearing John's oath. He was as much of a Secesh in sentiment as any of them and resented being excluded from their activities, whether he could ride or shoot or not. John had great misgivings that Lou already knew too much. He needed to find a way to include Lou so he wouldn't turn on them. Or at least make Lou think he was included. He didn't want to deceive his friend, but this was war, and war was hell—even if he never set foot on a battlefield.

CHAPTER 6

JOHN AND BOOTH became a common sight on the capital city's streets. Booth liked to work out in Brady's gymnasium, but John never did cotton to building burly muscles. They spent most evenings in saloons—Taltavul's next to Ford's Theater, or Deery's above the National, establishments that catered to a higher class of clientele. John strutted about town, head high, basking in his new status as a member of the elite.

Between drinks, the pair frequented Barker's Shooting Gallery at Eleventh and Pennsylvania. Booth was an expert marksman, from any position, a perfectionist. No one could keep up with him—except John—who'd been shooting since he could walk. His Pa saw to that.

Unlike the more deliberate Booth, John was a quick snap-shot. His accuracy was about two-thirds of Booth's, but John was a natural shooter. Booth was a student—he had to practice. They appeared as exact opposites—John was as reserved and tall as Booth was rambunctious and a head shorter. But both men could shoot the base off a wine bottle—through the neck, leaving it pristine. John cleverly pulled his shots ever so slightly whenever Booth had a bad outing.

Hearing nothing from his job application to the War Department, John took a clerking position at Adams Express Company, a private package service. He was a hard, meticulous worker—when he worked. His mind wandered much of the time. Would Booth's nefarious, and admittedly insane plot work, or would they all be thrown into the pokey? But something kept him from backing out—besides his devotion to the South—the excitement, the thrill of being embroiled in a plot that would change the course of history. It was drastic enough to be effective in forcing the North to release those prisoners the South so desperately needed. After he'd gotten over the initial shock of what Booth planned to do—after all, John's assignments had never involved any position approaching the presidency—it started to make more sense. As they'd discussed many times at home, Abraham Lincoln deserved everything he had coming to him from this war he started. And what was fairer than an even exchange?

Now he needed a few days off. His respectable but mundane job had to take a back seat. When he asked his boss, Charles Dunn, for several days' leave, Dunn blinked in bafflement. Leave was unheard of, especially for one who'd just been hired.

"Why do you need leave so soon?" he asked John. "You just started working here."

"Well, my mother has to travel into Charles County, Maryland, and she needs my escort for her own protection. It's dangerous there for a woman—Rebel raiders and all—why, I hear tell that there ain't seven loyal Union men in the whole county—and I know the roads. She does not, doncha see?"

He shook his head before John finished talking. "I cannot assent to such an action, Mr. Surratt. I'm sorry, but the answer is no." He dismissed John with a casual wave.

But John knew what was more important.

He went to Part Tobacco the next day, after leaving his mother at the tavern to settle her disintegrating monetary affairs. A neighbor, John Nothey, owed her some much-needed money. She relentlessly pursued the Nothey debt, and planned to make as many visits to Surrattsville as possible in order to collect. But it got her out of the stinking city, and the trips also made good cover for her support of pro-Confederate activities in aid of the Lincoln kidnapping plot. Just in case anyone investigated, she could say she was out of town, when she was really helping her son and his cohorts out.

Like John, she harbored a thrill at being involved in The Cause, marginal as her involvement was.

As the Surratts drove into Southern Maryland, Booth went to Baltimore to round up two friends, Samuel Arnold and Michael O'Laughlin, along with a trunk of munitions he'd fetched in New York. Arnold and O'Laughlin, ex-soldiers from the First Maryland Infantry, came into Washington City the next day, driving Booth's horse and buggy. That night, after trying to convince them how fair and just the plan was, Booth took them to Ford's Theater and stationed them at a back exit to show them how physically feasible it was, too.

"It is to be done next Wednesday," Booth laid out his plans, "at the performance of *Jack Cade*, one of

Lincoln's favorite plays. The tyrant is sure to show, and another man, John, will be up to help. A theater helper, Edman Spangler, will turn down the gas at a signal from me. The play is full of shouting and fury. That will help cover any struggle in the box."

Arnold and O'Laughlin exchanged glances. "I see this scheme's weaknesses from the get-go, Booth. You presume too much." Arnold shook his head. "You assume that people will react as you expect."

"Yeah," O'Laughlin concurred. "All it would take is one man of courage to get up on that stage to delay us long enough for someone else to run out and fetch the police or the provost marshal."

"Hell, no!" Booth stomped his foot. "We'll hit them so hard and fast, they'll be stupefied. You can count on it," he promised. "Besides, I purchased two extra horses for two of us to be outriders. And there will be relay mounts down at Tee Bee."

"Whatever," Arnold said without conviction. He knew damn well that wasn't gonna happen. So why argue with the arrogant actor? He just wanted to stick around and see Booth fail.

In Port Tobacco, John set up the crossing of the Potomac and met with Thomas Harbin, who'd been in direct touch with Confederate Secretary of State and spymaster Judah Benjamin. John then met Eddy Martin. Martin was there to cross the Potomac, purchase cotton and tobacco from the South, and spirit them North.

John knew this was illegal, but it was part of a Lincoln program to finance the war. The old baboon designed it to keep Northern spinning mills open and provide export income to offset the horrendous outflow of capital from the North to Europe to finance the war. Martin was engaged in a sort of legal illegality with administration approval. Hundreds of men, civilian and military, representing the Treasury and War Departments, were now engaged in similar operations, some official and some private, but all for profit.

"Do you know much about the crossing of the Potomac from here?" Martin asked John.

"A little," he replied with caution, "but I've never done it myself. It's illegal to run the blockade, you know. That's what all those warships steaming up and down the river are for." John decided to cover himself with innocence and the obvious until he could feel out Martin and decide what he was about.

"Well, I've hired that damned little Dutchman, I thought he was a Russian, but others say no, to put me across. I've been paying him good money for extra consideration, but he's been delaying me with nonsense excuses." Martin's irritated tone matched his scowl.

John wasn't a bit surprised. "Are we talking about Atzerodt?"

"You know him?"

"Heck, yeah." John flicked his wrist. "Everyone around here does. But he's German. He's a carriage painter by trade. Lives with his concubine outside town. Never married. They have a child, I believe."

Martin's eyes narrowed. "Can he be trusted?" Doubt crept into his voice.

"Sure...for the right price. Maybe you haven't reached it yet. Blockade-running is a dangerous piece of work, you know," he warned. "Just be patient. This is a busy place."

"Hrrmph," Martin mumbled as he shuffled off.

What a slipshod operation this is turning out to be. John shook his head, stupefied. Booth's "friends" from Baltimore hesitant to act in capturing Lincoln and looking for the smart-aleck Booth to fail, a Yankee government selling out to their own corruptionists for cotton profits to keep Northern and British mill hands from rioting in the streets for bread, the Confederate government spending a rumored million and a half in gold to finance it all...to what end? John rubbed his temples, as this mess made his head hurt. *Is everybody crazy?*

A sudden stab of fear nearly knocked John off his feet. *Can I be considered criminal—or even insane—to be involved in this mess for the self-determination of Southern whites?* His mind wandered as his pulse quickened. *And a war of white men all over the enslavement or freedom of black folk, who would be denied equality by both sides no matter who won?* He pushed his eagerness and patriotism aside and questioned his judgment, his mental stability. Then he pictured the South reveling in victory over those damn Yankees, their soldiers marching home in glory. The fear gave way to a new spark of excitement akin to arousal. Since he agreed to participate in this scheme, conflicting emotions pulled him in every direction. If only something—or someone—would determine his fate, with no looking back, no misgivings, no regrets.

He gazed into the heavens. "Oh, Pa, how I wish you were here."

~

"I'll be back tomorrow," John told innkeeper James Brawner. He then went to the farm of Mitchell Smoot for the night. Like everyone else in and around Port Tobacco, Smoot helped run the so-called Confederate secret mail line, the communications route both sides used to send mail and people between the North and South. Smoot had one of the biggest and stoutest boats in the region—just the thing for transferring a kidnapped president, his carriage, and Confederate abductors across the Potomac.

Smoot lived on the east side of the river. If John could buy Smoot's big boat and two others, Booth's plot could go into immediate operation. He'd already purchased a smaller skiff to be stationed in Goose Bay, a part of Port Tobacco Inlet.

"I'm using my boat right now. Can you not wait a while?" Smoot asked John.

"Not really." He shifted from foot to foot, too antsy to stand still. "I'll need to take possession right off. It's for The Cause, Mitch. I can't be more specific, but it's for an event of history-making magnitude, which will startle and astound the entire world." John shut his mouth before he said any more. *Am I starting to sound like Booth?* Great Scott, he couldn't let that happen. "Uh, what I meant to say was, no effort is too small for The Cause," he corrected himself quickly. "We need to win this war, and I'm danged if I won't do all it takes to win it."

Smoot spat on the ground. "Yup, I know whatch-'u're sayin' here, John," he grumbled.

So John hadn't needed to be cautious; Smoot well knew the score. The whole countryside from Port Tobacco to Washington City had been abuzz with the rumors of Lincoln's abduction for weeks. It amazed John how fast the gossip spread. But he didn't let the brassy scheme put him off. No deed of his lifetime would match this. Pushing aside his doubts and fears, he savored every minute, every whispered message, every secret closed-door drawn-drapes meeting at the boarding house.

Typical of secret operations in any Civil War, there was little or no security. So John wasn't surprised when word got around that Booth yapped to theater friends in city bars that something "big" was about to happen. With his newly acquired confidence and cocky gait, John sauntered into bars and did his own blabbing, but not to the degree Booth did. Bragging wasn't his nature. He kept the key facts to himself. He first confided in Joe Knott, barkeeper at the old family tavern in Surrattsville. But even Knott had nodded with a leer, telling John without a word he'd heard it already.

George Atzerodt told every soul in Port Tobacco, "I vill soon so rich be dat ven I back come, I dis whole goddamn town vill buy. Ja!"

Smoot now agreed, "All right, John. I will sell. But it will cost you $250, and not a penny less. I want no Confederate scrip or graybacks. I want gold Yankee dollars. Greenbacks will cost you twenty-five percent more. That's sixty—"

"No need to figure, Mitch." John concealed a grin as he stroked his whiskers. "Your terms are acceptable. Gold dollars it is. But I want to deposit the money with a trusted third party, to be paid when me and my companions decide to use the boat."

"I want half now, the rest put on deposit with Judge Stone in Port Tobacco. Deal?" he ventured.

John nodded. "Deal. You will turn the boat over to Atzerodt, and he will convey it to George Bateman over on King's Creek. Bateman will hide it at his place."

"When are you going to Richmond next?" Smoot asked.

"Oh, I wouldn't know much about that." John gave him an airy wave. "But if the Yankees knew what I've done or what I was doing, I'd stretch hemp, I mean to say." John jerked his head back, as if he had just dropped off the scaffold. Both men laughed with a slight undercurrent of unease. Sometimes a dose of gallows humor was a welcome break in the tension, the harsh uncertainty of what lay ahead. None of them knew what tomorrow would bring, so they took every chance to laugh it up now.

The following evening, Thomas Harbin came to see John at the Brawner House in Port Tobacco. Luckily John got to him before any of the bar flies cottoned on. Harbin slipped John a bulky package wrapped in plain paper and tied in a string. "Thanks, Tom. Good night." John didn't have to open it right away; he knew just what and how much it was: $300 in Confederate Secret Service funds, in Yankee greenbacks. Good thing the Reb government didn't mess with its own currency, preferring to operate in gold or Secretary Chase notes.

John met his fellow plotters in Washington two days later. Arnold and O'Laughlin seemed more skittish than ever. "Booth, this rain will muddy up the roads," Arnold whined. "They will be nothing but slimy rivers of muck. We could lose the whole coach in some of those Southern Maryland mud bogs."

John brought a new wrinkle in. "Listen, Booth, I just learnt something from Harbin in Port Tobacco. He told me that Richmond is sending a man up to help us subdue Lincoln. This fella is bigger and stronger than Ol' Abe. They want no harm to come to him during the abduction. Let's wait till he gets here."

"No, *you* listen, all of you!" Booth banged his walking stick on the floor. "We are going to strike while the iron is hot. That's now, tonight! I am fully capable of out-wrestling that son of a bitch in the White House. I have a covered coach available. We have the guns, accoutrements, ropes to tie across the roads and foul up the pursuit, and even a wrench to dismantle the coach so it will ride low and steady on the boat in the water," he recited as if from a script.

Arnold and O'Laughlin waited at the passageway, according to plan. Booth and John went in only to find that the Lincoln party had not shown. The night was too wet and raw to travel, so the old mule stayed home.

Back outside, Booth threw a conniption fit. "Damn that miserable bastard!" He flung his hat to the ground and stomped on it. "How dare he not show up to the greatest show of my...his life! I can just throttle him!" He made fists and twisted them in opposite directions, wringing an invisible neck.

John stared at Booth open-mouthed and wide-eyed, yet enthralled with the histrionic show of emotion. It was like watching one of his theatrical performances.

John didn't dare behave like that in front of others, even though he was as shattered as Booth was. He'd do his own ranting and raving alone in his room later.

"Calm down, Booth, we can plan another—um—abduction," John tried to appease his ringleader. Ignoring him, Booth climbed upon his mount, spurred it on and, kicking up swirls of dust, disappeared into the night.

John pondered the evening's events and voiced his concerns to the visibly relieved O'Laughlin and Arnold. "We need a more reliable notion of Lincoln's whereabouts. Booth is too much an ad lib idealist and not enough of a hard-nosed realist—he plays at being a villain, but this is real life. We must not approach villainy but personify it, or we'll chase Lincoln forever to no avail."

"Well, I'm not sure I want Booth to succeed at all," Arnold admitted. "This flash-in-the-pan stuff is a sure route to failure ending with everyone involved in jail—or swinging from the gallows."

"Yeah, there's always the grim gallows." John circled his neck with his fingers and shuddered.

After the failed attempt to kidnap Lincoln at Ford's Theater, John went to Baltimore with the $300 Harbin had slipped him. Wanting to make Lou feel wanted, but most of all, to prevent him from ratting them out, he brought his friend with him. But John insisted on leaving Lou in their room when he went to visit Judah Benjamin's henchman Lewis Powell at Miller's Hotel, one of Baltimore's many Confederate safe houses.

Booth had told him a few teaser snippets about Powell's background, and it captured his imagination. He listened enraptured, as he'd done when Ma read him tales as a child. But no one could make this stuff up. It was a miracle the fellow survived it all.

John knocked on the door and in a split second, he faced an inordinately powerful giant with a mop of black hair and a strong square jaw. His steely blue eyes stated: "Combat veteran. Don't mess with me." John had seen the type before. They spoke volumes, yet never seemed to see anything. But in reality, they missed nothing.

"Mr. Powell?" John said.

"I am him—uh, he," Powell answered.

"John Harrison." He used the alias he'd adopted for official spy business.

Powell beckoned John to enter and closed the door behind him. "Come Retribution," he announced.

"Complete Victory," came John's answer.

They shook hands.

"Good to see you, Powell. How are things going?" He stepped inside.

"Not bad." He smoothed his hair back from his forehead. "I've only been here a while. I couldn't get a room at Branson's. But I've been told I can move over there tomorra."

"Excellent. How are you and Parr doing?" John referred to the owner of Parr's China Halls, a store in downtown Baltimore that sold china—also a Confederate drop-off point for messages and people. Powell worked there as a cover. The huge lumbering soldier reminded John of the old saw about the bull in the china shop. If he busted anything, Parr would flat-out go haywire. "You two get along? He's kind of a crusty old coot."

"Yeah. He lets me work at the end of the day. I can do pretty much what I want otherwise. But I need money to pay my accounts. Here, siddown." Powell offered John a straight-backed chair and dragged one up for himself.

John knew how soldiers enjoyed telling war stories, and he couldn't wait to hear more. It would be even better coming from the veteran himself. "So I hear you're a vet of the first caliber. Where did you serve? Did you get wounded—or wound anyone?" He didn't want to flat out ask if he'd killed anyone. If Powell had, John was sure he'd brag about it.

"First I joined a hometown unit, the Hamilton Blues, which became part of the Second Florida infantry. Fought from Williamsburg, through the Seven Days, Second Manassas, Sharpsburg, Fredericksburg, Chancellorsville, Gettysburg—" He counted on his fingers—"and a half dozen other skirmishes in between, mostly in Perry's Brigade of Longstreet's Corps."

"Weren't you wounded at all?" John didn't see any scars and the soldier sure had all his limbs.

"Once." He rolled up his sleeve and bared his arm. "Flesh wound, lucky for me. I was captured at Gettysburg, but I escaped and returned South. Then I served for a spell with Gilmore's Maryland guerrilla cavalry, before winding up with Mosby's Forty-third Virginia Cavalry Battalion. From there, Mosby sent me to Secretary of War Benjamin as a combination spy, agent, and assassin. Then Benjamin sent me here."

John fought twinge of envy. Military service wasn't his calling, even if it led to glamorous spying—that's what he was doing anyways, and without having fought in two dozen battles! As for assassinating—he'd leave that to the experts. His courage stretched only so far.

"And here you are." John raised his hands and gestured around the room. "And here we are. So—Richmond sent me with $300 to give you. That will hold you for a while. Especially if you stay at Branson's. They do it for The Cause, never charge couriers and spies like us full fare."

"I was told that you would tell me what the plan was." Powell leaned forward, clasping his hands between his knees.

"In brief, it's to capture Abraham Lincoln, spirit him away to Richmond, and trade him for our prisoners of war held in the North." Now that he'd met Powell, John reckoned the trained assassin would find the whole thing child's play.

But Powell stared for a few beats, with those steely eyes that John couldn't read. As he began to expect Powell to turf him out, he displayed a grin. "This move would best Mosby's capturing a Union general out of his bed at Fairfax Court House and carrying him off through a ring of Federal soldier guards," he said. "How, when, and where are we to do it?"

John expelled a whoosh of relief that Powell was eager to jump in and join them. "That's not our concern," he replied firmly. "Our leader is developing the plan. You'll meet him in due time. I will say that we need you to hold Lincoln down and subdue him until we can handcuff him or tie him up. You look strong enough. The rest of us would have to take him all at once and might hurt him. Have you ever seen him lift an axe by swinging his arm from his waist to shoulder height? It's mighty hard to do."

Powell's eyes lit up. "So that's why Secretary Benjamin had me do that!"

"He did? If you can do that, you'll be able to restrain ol' Abe until we truss him up." John sat back and crossed his left ankle over his right knee. This brute was as good as on the team. "Well, that's all you need to know. I brought a friend, Louis Weichmann, who's awaiting me over at the Maltby House. An old school chum. He works in the Yankee War Department for the Commissary of Prisons. He's been giving us figures on where all our men are being held. He wants to do more, but he can't ride or shoot. Besides, the head man don't trust him. He's hoping to get an appointment to study for the priesthood here. But the appointment would come out of the Richmond diocese. The war don't stop everything, I s'pose." He gave a one-shoulder shrug. "So, just stick around, be available at the Branson House, and check in with Parr every day." He unfolded his frame and stretched as he stood. "You'll be got in touch with at the proper time. Reckon you can handle it?"

"Yep...Mr. Harrison? Please sit on the far side of the bed." Powell gestured with a meaty hand. "I want to show you something."

Giving Powell a quizzical look, John sat on the far side of the bed, the very far side, at the edge. *He don't look like a Nancy. But one never knows.* He already had his doubts about Lou. But Powell didn't sit down next to him. Brandishing a boastful grin, he grabbed the iron bedstead at the foot of the bed with both hands. He gave a little leap and extended his whole body out full length about two feet off the floor and parallel to it, much like a circus acrobat. Then he folded his legs to his waist and let himself slowly drop to the floor. "Strong enough for you?"

"Well, butter my hide and call me a biscuit!" John shook his head in wonder.

"Aw, it was nothin'. You should'a seen me lift a half dozen split chestnut fence rails up alone and then mount my horse and ride a mile with them in perfect balance before droppin' 'em over at a place in Warrenton."

"Whoa! Booth sure knows how to pick 'em! I'll be in touch, sir." John quit the room, closing the door behind him.

Walking down the street, looking for a café to take the edge off his appetite, he marveled at Powell's history, his military accomplishments, his raw strength. He could snap John in half like a twig. No wonder Booth picked him out of the crowd. John knew this plot couldn't fail at this point, drastic as it was. Not with somebody like Powell keeping things in order. He only hoped Booth's other cohorts were half as capable. The team was almost complete—Booth and John as the brains, and Powell as the brawn. But they needed more brawn—they had plenty of brains.

CHAPTER 7

"Sorry we left you wondering what was gonna happen," John told Powell on the second visit to the Surratt rooming house. "We had to get approval from the high command in Canada. They manage the Secret Service operations now. Richmond communicates with them and they talk to us. Sometimes the boys in Canada act on their own. I'm the courier between them."

"So when do we move?" Powell's voice carried an edge of impatience.

"I know how you feel, pal. I'm coiled up and ready to spring, too. But I'm not sure yet. It depends on what Lincoln does. Whether he gives us an opportunity. Whether we can assemble our crew fast enough. I reckon mid-March, give or take a day or two. I'm sending a telegram to Parr asking you to come to the city. It'll be on a moment's notice. So be ready. Your answer must read, '*she* will be over' and give a time of day you'll arrive on the cars. Go to the Surratt boarding house on the corner of H and Sixth, and give your name as the Reverend Louis Paine. You are to be a Baptist lay preacher—like your daddy back home. My Ma will be expecting you. She's Mrs. Surratt." He turned to leave. "I'll contact you there. Meanwhile I'm off to Canada delivering dispatches."

As he had indicated to Powell, he'd had a busy week, with courier trips on the north side of the Potomac, between the river and Washington City.

After a night at Spottswood Hotel, John reported to the Confederate State Department. He followed the instructions in the *Stranger's Guide to Richmond* he found in the lobby. *The Secretary's Office is in the front part of the Treasury Building. Ascend by the stairs at end of passage leading from Bank Street entrance. First door on east side of passage at head of stairs.*

"Surratt," he announced to the Assistant Secretary of State, Quinton Washington.

"Oh, yes, Mr. Surratt. Please. Come on in. Secretary Benjamin is waiting for you." Washington opened the door to the State Department's inner sanctum.

"Mr. Surratt, Secretary Benjamin."

"How do you do?" The portly Benjamin rose from the black walnut table heaped with stacks of papers. To John, the best word to describe him was *rabbinical,* with a round face framed in a beard, curly black hair, and a smile that beamed friendship and welcome. John heard he'd once called himself the Confederacy's "court Jew," much like his medieval Sephardic ancestors. But John thought his features revealed a sort of smarminess, like a drummer, as traveling salesmen were called. His handshake was a mite limp, too, like most politicians, having grasped too many constituents' extended hands.

"Please sit down. Drink, Surratt? We have some

excellent sherry for this time of the war." He gestured at a half-empty bottle. "Recently in from the blockade, you know."

"Thanks much, sir, but I'll pass," John refused politely. Brandy he'd have accepted. Even whiskey. "To me, sherry's a cross between beeswax and the cola syrup my Ma gave me for catarrh as a young'un. No offense, sir."

"None taken." Benjamin's tone implied *that's all the more for me* as he poured himself a glassful and kept the bottle well within reach.

"Very well, let's get right to business." Benjamin clasped his fingers around his glass. "You come very well recommended by our men in Confederate Maryland. Their names are not important." Benjamin grinned as he wagged his hand dismissively, but John knew their names. He figured Benjamin just wanted to cover his hide. But that was fine by him—it showed integrity—and the sense to keep his trap shut about certain things.

"As you may be aware, Mr. Surratt, the Confederacy is in rather dire straits. General Grant has kept Richmond and Petersburg under constant siege since last summer. Our other armies have been driven back all over the South. General Sherman is marching through the Carolinas to our rear. If we are to survive another year, we must alter our strategy to face these realities." Benjamin paused and took a long pull of his drink. John watched him nearly drain the glass. *So much for sherry being a sipping spirit.*

"Our campaign for 1865 is to be an innovative approach to modern warfare. First, we proposed last fall to spend one and a half million dollars in gold to finance a massive campaign behind the Union battle

lines involving sabotage, the instigation of disturbances against the Northern military draft..." He took
a breath and another pull of his sherry, "...introducing
infectious diseases into selected Union cities, destroying New York City by arson, and capturing Lincoln and holding him hostage to free Confederate
prisoners up North. That's where you come in, you
and Mr. Booth." He looked John in the eye. "We have
decided to support your little group in its efforts to
capture Lincoln and bring him South along the secret
line for barter. It was scouted by the late Lieutenant
Bowie last fall—I believe you may've known him?
The idea is to free all of our veteran soldiers and win
the war."

"Excuse me, sir." John held up his hand. "I'm
your man, you know that. But let me play devil's ad-
vocate a moment here. Suppose Lincoln refuses to
negotiate? Or even more likely, what if the Yankee
government does not want him back? A lot of Republicans would just as soon bid him good riddance—look
at the election last fall. Several attempts were made to
deny him the nomination and the election. That's if I
read the newspapers right and they were telling the
truth."

"You did, and they were." Benjamin knocked
back the last of his drink. "We thought of that angle,
too. It's quite possible that Grant will try to outflank
us toward the South Side Railroad, while Lincoln refuses to cooperate. General Lee plans to launch a pre-
emptive attack to slap him back and then do what the
Yankees and most Southerners thought impossible—
evacuate Richmond." He poured himself a refill and
continued, "We plan to do it during the wettest
month of the year in these parts—April. The idea is

for General Lee's men to head west along the railroad toward Amelia Court House, tearing the tracks up as they pass. This will leave the Union army in the mud floundering toward their wartime goal of Richmond." He gestured at the bottle. "You sure you don't want none? It's a mite more tasty than beeswax."

"Never touch the stuff." John waved it off.

Benjamin imbibed and went on, "Meanwhile, General Lee will turn south on the cars and join with General Johnston in North Carolina. Their combined armies will attack and defeat Sherman, then turn north, leaving a small holding force behind to contain him. They'll meet Grant coming southward, all strung out along the impossible roads, and defeat him in detail before he can unite his forces. Since Lee and Johnston will be between Grant and Sherman, they can turn and pummel the one that needs it most, re-pummel and re-re-pummel."

"You sure have this well planned." John glowed with confidence hearing it from Benjamin, rather than the impetuous, limelight-hogging Booth. Even with his doubts and skepticism, it made sense.

Benjamin nodded. "Your specific assignment is to carry dispatches explaining our campaign to our agents in Montreal. Then you are to return and assist in the capture of Lincoln. We already sent a man, Powell, to Baltimore. He will come back to Washington City and assist you when you and Booth are ready to move. Any more questions?"

"No, sir. I already met Powell. But I need more specific instructions on who to contact in Montreal."

"All of that will be given to you by Mr. Washington on your way out." Benjamin stood and John followed his lead. "Well, good day—and good luck."

Benjamin extended his hand and John shook it. "The hopes of the entire South ride with you in your quest, young man."

～

Later, after John left, Quinton Washington entered Benjamin's office.

"So, what do you think of our new messenger?" Benjamin asked.

"I dunno," Washington pondered. "Nice fella, but he seems unusually mutton-headed for his role to me. Asked too many questions—slow to catch on."

"I must presume you're wrong." Benjamin drummed his fingers on the desk. "The smart ones ask all the questions, so he seemed intelligent to me. Cautious—not an eager beaver jumping all over it. He weighed the possible consequences. You think *he* seemed mutton-headed? You should see the rest o'that nitty gritty band. Sheesh. But they're all we got for this dicey operation. The smart ones just run the blockade."

～

Samuel Arnold and Michael O'Laughlin became more and more isolated from the Confederate underground in Washington City as Federal spies and detectives tracked their every movement. The federal officers stood outside Parr's China Halls and the Branson Rooming House, taking copious notes on everyone who patronized these places. They talked to the hired servants at Branson's and waited for "John Harrison" to return.

But he did not. Parr had used another Rebel contact, liquor dealer Jacob Heim, to send a trunk of provisions received from Booth's actor friend, John Mathews, to Dr. Mudd as instructed. He heard nothing else. Finally, Parr sent Lewis Powell to the Surratts to find out what was happening. He went as "Mr. James Wood," an alias that Mary Surratt would recognize, if John was not at home.

He was not. But Mary reassured Mr. Wood, "All is on schedule. Wait for the telegram from John to come south and join in the plot. Patience is the word." She put Wood up for one night in an attic room. He disappeared the next morning, too early for the suspicious Lou Weichmann to take up his prying questioning of the night before.

Lou paced the floor of his room, fuming. Booth, Herold, Atzerodt, in and out all hours of the day and night. Everyone wanting to talk with John. Now this Wood character. If they didn't talk to John, they talked to his mother. Behind closed doors—closed to him. Yet they'd cajoled him into giving them information on Confederate prisoners held in the North. But when Lou asked Booth or John, "Can I ride with you, please, can I?" they gave him the same old rebuff, "No, you cannot ride or shoot."

Nor could he learn to ride or shoot at this late date. So, after a plea to God for courage, Lou made the most crucial decision of his life—to turn them in. This tore him up inside, for he loved John like a brother. But it was the Christian thing to do. It broke his heart that John didn't return his fondness and loyalty. It wasn't John's fault—he'd become a Booth bootlicker, just like the rest of them. The whole family fawned over the overrated matinee idol—

Annah made a prat out of herself, blushing and giggling behind her hand every time he showed up. And as for Mrs. Surratt, she dolled herself up like a tart for him—rouge, powder, tulips in her hair—revolting! Everything was *Booth this, Booth that*. As the only household member who hadn't fallen under the actor's phony spell, he couldn't stand hearing the name. All Boothed out, he'd never attend another of their plays either.

~

"Major Gleason," Lou addressed his office head in a hushed tone, "could I meet you in the supply room in a few minutes? I have something very confidential to consult with you on."

"Go sit down and get back to work, Weichmann," came the curt reply.

D. H. L. Gleason was a combat veteran of the 1st Massachusetts Volunteer Cavalry. He had been discharged because of wounds and was technically a civilian, but smart subordinates referred to him by his brevet rank of major—and he'd earned it.

Lou knew Gleason considered him to be intellectually capable, an excellent clerk. He admired Lou's education, his ability to speak several languages. But Gleason considered him a coward, Lou learned when he overheard, "and in bravery I should call him a dwarf." Lou never called him on it—he wanted to keep his job.

Lou turned and slunk out, but Gleason called out, "No, wait...I need some help in the supply room. Come with me." He limped to the large closet nearby, his movement hampered by a gunshot wound to his hip.

In the supply room, as an oil lamp sucked up the stuffy air, Gleason turned to Lou. "So, what is it? Does this have anything to do with that crack the other day to the other clerks that you could make $30,000 any day you wanted?" The scar on his head from a saber cut gleamed in the flickering lamplight.

"No, sir." He pulled a grimy handkerchief from his trouser pocket and mopped his sweaty brow. "I was just blowing a lot of balderdash. Trying to honey-fuggle them."

"I thought so." Gleason smirked. "The only place I know where a body can make that kind of swag is in running the blockade or something more dangerous."

Lou didn't conceal his look of misery. Rivulets of sweat ran down his back, and it had nothing to do with the stuffy room.

Expelling a ragged breath, he shook more than on the night he begged John to help with The Cause. This was at least as important. "Sir—I harbor a terrible secret." Lou kept his voice businesslike, and forced the emotion away. "It so weighs on me that I must confide in someone. I need to tell it to you, but only under the strictest pledge of secrecy. You must promise to keep it mum by your oath as an officer and a gentlemen."

"Forget it." Gleason held up his hands to halt any further pleas. "I don't want to hear any of this 'secret' bunkum. I'm too busy to play games." Gleason picked up a ream of paper and headed back to his office, leaving Lou standing there sweating, but oddly relieved. Maybe this rebuff was a sign from God...to shut up about it. God Himself would punish the conspirators for their sins.

But after Lou slept on it and prayed on it once more, he considered it his patriotic duty as a Christian to carry out God's work. Back he went the next day, pleading with Major Gleason in the hall. "Please, sir, respect my confidence!"

"Aw'right!" Gleason threw his hands up. "Providing that I can do so safely without endangering the war effort or any other person," he said, his voice weary.

Without preamble, Lou spewed out, "I often tell my co-workers that Mrs. Surratt's boarding house, where I live, is a rendezvous for Southerners and Rebel sympathizers, who come and go at all times, day and night."

"Yeah, yeah." Gleason rolled his eyes heavenward. "You've kept us entertained for some time now. It's really good for the moral spirits of the men to laugh at *something* in this war."

"No, no. Please, bear with me." He slowed the pace of his speech. "Information is gathered and given out, and only well-known, disloyal people are welcome there."

"You better stop to think what you just said about *yourself*." Gleason stared Lou down. "Frankly, if you hadn't joined the clerks' militia and attended all the drill meetings to defend the city against potential Rebel attack, I would have a great deal of doubt about you."

Lou returned the stare and declared, "Yes, in fact, they *do* suspect me, and only the old-time friendship between John Surratt and me makes it possible for me to stay. For some time, I've been aware that something covert is going on behind closed doors. Visitors have long secret meetings in John's room. Mrs. Surratt, the actor John Wilkes Booth, and some other suspicious-looking characters are always there. I'm sure they're connected with the Rebel government and use false names. John quarreled with me the other day for commenting on Booth's frequent visits, and made me swear not to reveal anything I knew or might learn. I cannot hold it inside any longer, and I know you will stand by me now I have told you." There. It was out—in the hands of fate. A tight knot in the back of his neck seemed to untie itself. But growing anticipation made his heart pound. "Well?" he blurted out, anxiety churning inside him.

Gleason looked away, snorted and chuckled. To Lou it sounded more cynical than mildly amused. Wasn't he getting through?

"Listen to this," he rattled on, more out of nervousness than a need to reveal more. "John told me they were engaged in running cotton from the South into our lines, as a blind, that they had planned to kidnap Mr. Lincoln and his cabinet, take them over the Potomac into Rebel territory, and thus force the North to compromise with the South. If they could not effect an advantageous compromise, they would hold them for a large ransom—"

"Oh, hell," Gleason broke in, "they can have the sons of bitches for free as far as I'm concerned. Then maybe we can get rid of their milk-water policies. That's my take on the whole damned thing." He turned to leave.

But Lou refused to give up at this point. He grabbed Gleason's arm and turned the major to face him. "The time set is Inauguration Day, March fourth, as there will be so many strangers in the city that people's attention will be diverted, and this will give them a better chance to operate." Desperate to persuade the man, never before was he more determined to sway someone. Even his numerous applications to schools and job positions paled in comparison with this. A positive outcome to this could make him a hero!

"They should have the common sense to operate when there are fewer people around, if they want to spirit someone out of the city," Gleason argued.

"Hear me out, sir," Weichmann begged. "Please."

He eyed Lou suspiciously. "There's more?"

"Lots. These men have arranged with Rebels across the Potomac to have men and horses ready there, to get the captives to Richmond as quickly as possible," he blathered on. "John has shown me letters alleged to be from officials in the Rebel government—but he would not show me the signatures. He said all arrangements had been made, and they only waited for March fourth. There was not the slightest chance of failure, and now the time is drawing near to act, if act they do." He gulped. "Now, sir, you know my trouble, and I feel you can and will help me, but you must be discreet. Don't speak to me on the street, as I am watched and by those who would swear my life away to help the South."

Gleason tilted his head, eyes focused on Lou. "Is this legit, Weichmann? You're not pulling my leg? Or something else?" He sounded on the brink of being convinced now.

Lou emptied his lungs in relief, but what he really wanted was to empty was his bladder.

"No, sir, I swear it's all true, every word. I don't

lie. It's the Eleventh Commandment to me, and I follow all the Commandments." He couldn't keep the pleading out of his voice, past caring how pathetic he sounded. "Please, sir, the future of the South depends on this conversation."

"Then go over to the Provost Marshal's Office and tell them. Tell General Augur, who commands the city."

"No, no!" He shook his head, wiping spittle from his lips. "That would be too risky. They would find out and kill me sure." His voice quivered as he trembled in terror.

"Can't you join this group?" Gleason egged him on. "You live in the same damn house."

Lou averted his eyes, embarrassed to tell Gleason how many times he'd begged John to no avail. "They haven't asked me to join. Well, not really. John knows how busy I am with my job. None of these other men have real jobs. They're just loafers, and have all the time in the world to sit around and conjure up madcap schemes to ruin the North. I, on the other hand, have a responsible job here, which I take very seriously." He raised his chin. Why not throw in a word about how much he valued his job here? It might come in handy at promotion time.

"My advice is to wangle your way in." Gleason wiggled his hands like swimming fish. "Find out what they're up to and expose them at the proper moment. Talk 'secesh' to them. You can do it. You're a fast enough talker. You can gab the hind legs off a donkey." He gave Lou a half-smirk.

Lou took that as a backhanded compliment. "I fear they're too sharp for that, sir." The cockiness drained from his voice. "But I'll try."

Defeat crushed him as he retreated down the hall. After all that, Gleason wanted *him* to thwart this intricate plot. How could one person against the five or six of those lunatics accomplish anything? He hadn't even offered any assistance. It made Lou wonder if Gleason believed him after all. If this was a big joke to the major, the joke would be on the North in the end. Booth, that fiend with a heart as black as hell, was serious about carrying out his plot, and Lou had to find somebody in this bloody government who would take it seriously.

But meanwhile, he began devising ways to "wangle in" as Gleason put it. He knew Booth and his cohorts weren't flush with cash; he could wipe out his savings and donate to the plot. *Could I learn to shoot within a week after all?* he challenged himself. *Maybe I could at that. Booth can shoot, and he's even a bit Nancyish.*

Without even going home to his much-anticipated dinner, he headed straight over to McGuire's shooting gallery. Time was of the essence; he couldn't waste another minute.

~

That evening, Major Gleason went back to the rooming house he shared with Joshua Sharp, an assistant provost marshal. Gleason knew his levelheaded roommate would listen to the Weichmann tale and give a valuable opinion. But Sharp burst out laughing even before Gleason finished. Seeing the absurdity of it as he repeated it, Gleason began to chuckle, too.

"Pshaw! That's pure unadulterated hogwash."

Sharp guffawed. "I've heard conspiracy theories before, but this one takes the cake—and the cherry on top. Who is this Weichmann clown anyway?"

"He's a valued employee, reliable enough. I've never seen him go off the deep end—well, not before this, anyway. Never seemed to lack in the credibility department. I agree it sounds farfetched, but who the hell knows? Lincoln does have his enemies." Gleason paced the creaky floor, head down. "I wouldn't put it past Jeff Davis to cook up with something like this and round up a gaggle of bootlickers to carry out the dirty work. I'm on the fence about it myself. Only because it sounds so absurd, it could be true," he thought out loud. But he couldn't keep a straight face.

"To kidnap Lincoln and his whole cabinet yet?" Sharp lit a segar and spat out the end. "What would that accomplish? It borders on the farcical."

Gleason nodded, inhaling the rich tobacco aroma. "Yeah, you're right. Hell, they could barely get them across the Eastern Branch, much less the Potomac. I can see if it was a regiment of soldiers, but this motley crew—nah, not a chance. There must be a hundred Lou Weichmanns running around spreading conspiracy theories to whoever is dumb enough to listen."

Sharp smirked. "Like you, for instance?"

"Hardly," he retorted in a haughty tone. "I shut him up mighty quick. He wanted to babble more, but I had to get back to reality. I've had enough fairy tales." He turned to leave. "See you after the evening meal. Maybe we can play a few hands of knuckle-knuckle." So he had his second opinion. But he wasn't taking any chances. He'd let Weichmann think he wasn't interested, but he wouldn't let the matter peter out. He had the strangest hunch something lurked behind it—Weichmann may have exaggerated about seizing the entire cabinet, but Gleason wouldn't dare ignore it altogether.

He planned to speak with a co-worker, Major John Martin, who had connections directly to Secretary of War Stanton. The higher up, the better. If the bigshots blew it off, why, he'd forget about it. But he wanted to see if Martin would guffaw his way through it or take some action.

CHAPTER 8

"Well, what did Stanton say?" Gleason asked Martin a few days later. "Was he impressed?"

"Nah." Martin waved it off. "Stanton told me that rag-tag crew couldn't hurl a rotten tomato at the president without missing, much less kidnap him, on Inauguration Day or any other day, for that matter. If it wouldn't have ruined his reputation for sobriety, I suspect he would have laughed."

The idea of War Secretary Stanton finding humor in any situation sent both men into fits of laughter. And after the Inauguration passed without incident, they laughed even more.

So much for Louis Weichmann's credibility, Gleason scoffed, keeping a mental note of who'd move up in the ranks at promotion time.

A few days later, after Lou got home from work, John entered the room they shared and flopped down on the bed without a word. The old frame shook and squeaked.

Lou braced himself to keep from falling off. "John! Glad to see you home." But that was an understatement. He hadn't seen John for two whole days. It agitated his already-mixed feelings about ratting out his friend to the government, his back-and-forth rationalizing about saving the nation, and hoping John was Christian enough to forgive him.

"I'm tuckered out, Lou. I spent all day down country avoiding Federal cavalry." John covered his eyes with his arm, sounding half asleep.

Lou wanted to probe further, but by now knew John didn't share details. Broad strokes were all he got these days. "Sure. Will it bother you if I write a letter?"

"Not in the least," he murmured.

As Lou opened a bottle of ink and dipped his pen, a click of hardware sounded, and the door swung open. In lumbered the hulking Lewis Powell, now playing the role of Reverend Paine wearing a white collar—but of course it was dirty. He'd arrived last evening with that alias and the same dirty collar. Mrs. Surratt had given him the attic room again, where he'd stayed before as Mr. Wood. Lou knew danged well he was Powell; he didn't have a twin running around. He'd seen him at the house a few times when he peeked into the parlor during one of their "secret" meetings. He'd heard John call him "Mr. Powell" and introduce him to Annah that way. So who was he fooling, parading as a Reverend? It was blasphemous. Lou even prayed for the troubled man's soul.

"Is this Mr. Surratt?" Powell asked Lou.

"He sure looks like Mr. Surratt to me." Lou let the intruder know he was no simpleton. John raised up on one elbow, now wide-eyed and alert.

"I would like to talk privately with Mr. Surratt." Powell held the door wide open, presumably for Lou to beat a hasty exit. How subtle. Lou did not like people who entered rooms without knocking. He looked over at John for support, but got none. John nodded toward the open door, as much as to say he was sorry, but Lou had to leave. Knowing discretion was the better part of valor, he swallowed his pride and strode out, shooting Powell a dirty look.

"That's the fella I told you about up in Baltimore —the one our leader don't trust," John warned when they were alone. "You want to be careful what you say around him."

"Yeah, I figgered as much when I seen him hoverin' around in the hallway tryin'a glom our first meeting in the parlor. That's why I got up and closed the door. But he seems to favor your sister a lot." Powell plopped down on the bed uninvited. It sagged under his weight.

"God's bodkins, don't tell her that." John cringed. "She told me flat out she fights the urge to upchuck around the man, always grousing about how greasy and blubbery he is. She calls him 'Fatty,' among other less flattering names."

"I reckon he didn't like it last night when she played the piano and I sang along. One song was a mite spooky—something about a Hindoo." Powell sat back against the headboard and swung his feet up onto the bed, muddy boots and all.

"You mean 'Hindoo Mother.'" John nodded. "It's a family favorite, especially with Annah. By the bye, I hear you made quite a hit with the women. But Mrs. Holohan thinks you're not sanctimonious enough for a Baptist preacher—card playing? Euchre? Come now." He gave his cohort a sly smile.

Powell snickered. "Yeah, I gotta watch my step. Wanna see the fake moustachios I have for throwing off the Feds?" Powell pulled a hairy item out of his pocket. It looked like some sort of bug, all rumpled up and sticking to itself with spirit gum. He tossed it on the table next to Lou's letter.

John laughed at the flapdoodle. Powell wearing a disguise? Who did he think he'd bamboozle?

"I'd grow a real one, but I think facial hair looks scruffy." Powell's gaze landed on John's goatee. "On me, that is."

"Well, it makes me look older, and I need all the help I can get." John stroked his sparse whiskers. "So, did you bring the guns and such?"

"They're up in my garret room. Let's go take a look." He jerked his thumb in the direction of the door.

With John bringing up the rear, Powell clamored up the steep stairs to the third floor. They entered the small room and John shut the door behind them. Powell opened his carpetbag and dumped its contents on the bed.

"I had all this in my coat pockets last night to keep —what do you call him?—Puggy from seeing it."

"Fatty," John corrected him. "But Puggy will suffice in a pinch."

"Yeah, the nosy sum'bitch just had to carry it up. But I was ready for him." Powell grinned. In the half-light of the garret, his limestone-flecked teeth looked downright evil. John shuddered, thankful he was on their side.

~

Down in the parlor, Lou sat alone, fists clenched, seething. *This is all part of some play acting,* he mused silently. *Paine knows who John is and John knows him. John expected him to come sometime that afternoon! They were trying to deceive me!* Lou's anger bristled. He struck the sofa arm. *I'll show them!* He quit the parlor to go fetch his letter and writing materials. He wanted to finish it before dinner. "Those two had enough privacy, by God." He took the stairs two at a time. "It's *my* room, too."

Lou threw open the door and stalked inside. Instead of facing confrontation, he faced an empty room, his letter and writing implements where he'd left them. He sat down and reached for his pen, but froze. There, on the edge of the table, lay something gruesome. At first he thought it to be some sort of creepy crawler and reached for his shoe to squish it. But closer examination showed it to be—"Huh?" A false moustache!

"What in the Devil?" Lou swore aloud, then blessed himself. He examined the moustache, black and sticky on the back side from spirit gum. He decided he would make Paine sweat—surely the item was his. He secreted it in a small box on the desk where he stored personal items. Lou sat there a few moments, wondering where John and the interloper had gone. They couldn't have come down the stairwell. He would have heard them from his place of exile in the parlor. Upstairs! The garret room where Paine slept. Of course!

Lou entered the hall and started climbing the

stairs, slowly and stealthily this time. The door into the anteroom stood ajar. He craned his neck to peek inside, the same way he'd hovered around the parlor doorway that night of their meeting. All three garret room doors were shut, but voices floated to the rear. *What's sauce to the goose is sauce to the gander,* Lou affirmed to himself. He opened the door to Paine's room without knocking.

Paine leapt to his feet from the edge of the bed, revolver in hand. Multiple clicks broke the silence, as the bogus minister skillfully cocked the weapon. He sure didn't look the part of a mild Baptist pastor now. He bared his teeth like a feral animal. John, sitting on the bed, scrambled to cover up what lay between them, but not in time. Several pairs of sparkling new spurs, two Bowie knives, and at least one more handgun lay spread out in plain sight.

But the two conspirators relaxed as they realized who had intruded so unexpectedly.

"Oh, it's only *you*, Lou," John said almost too calmly. "Come on in."

Lou just stood there, paralyzed by fright. He still desperately wanted to be a part of everything—but this? Lou never considered the implications of John's involvement. Guns meant violence, possibly murder!

"S-s-sorry," he stammered. He backed out into the anteroom, slammed the door and stumbled down the stairs. He didn't stop at his bedroom, which had been so precious to him just minutes before, but hastened down to the first floor, frantic to find Mrs. Surratt.

He found her in the pantry off the kitchen. "Mrs. Surratt!" he gasped, panting with exertion. "I just saw John up in the attic with the *Reverend* Mr. Paine.

They have pistols, Bowies, and spurs. What is happening?" His words rushed out in one breath. "You must take action!"

"Tut tut now, Mr. Weichmann." She waved a dismissive hand, her words implying *mind your own beeswax, Fatty*. "Let us not go off half-cocked. Why would they *not* have arms and spurs? After all, they ride in the country a lot and it's very dangerous out there. They must have the means of self-protection."

"But—but—" Through his sputtering he couldn't believe her blasé attitude. "But—"

He followed her into the parlor. "But don't you see—"

"Sit down, Mr. Weichmann, rest a while." She pushed him down into an overstuffed chair. "It will be supper time soon. You'll feel much better after we all eat a little."

Still too jittery to relax, he sat at the edge of the chair and retrieved a piece of the newspaper, but it blurred before his eyes. Fiddling with the tassel on the cushion, he turned as footsteps pounded down the hall stairway. The door opened and in came John.

"Sorry if we startled you." He approached Lou. "Look what I have here. It's from Mr. Booth. A ten-dollar ticket to Ford's Theater for tonight's performance of *Jane Shore*."

Lou stood and playfully plucked the ticket from John's hand. "I am going, too!"

"Oh, no. No, you may not go." John swatted Lou on the arm in a boyish way and snatched the ticket back.

"Why not? Aren't we friends?" He rubbed his smarting arm.

"Certainly, but it's a personal matter. No offense implied," he hastened to add. "I'm taking the young ladies of the house."

"And the Reverend Mr. Paine?" Lou inwardly scolded himself for saying that. He made it so patently obvious that he was jealous of how that phony Reverend monopolized John's time—time that had been Lou's for so long. But he couldn't help it. He was losing the only friend he'd ever had to this wacky plot. He wished he could shake some sense into John so he'd abandon it all.

"Why, in fact, the Reverend Paine is going, too." John fluttered the ticket like a lady's fan. "While we're on the subject, might he borrow your blue military cloak for the evening?"

No, no! Lou wanted to scream. *No invitation and borrowing my good cloak! What kind of hypocrite are you, John?* But then Lou stopped himself, seeing a speck of comic relief amidst all this lunacy. Maybe Paine wanted to wear his false moustache to the theater. Let him try to find *that!*

"Yes, that will be all right," Lou gave in, knowing if he refused, he would alienate John even further.

Although Mary Holohan declined to go, Honora and Polly excitedly prepared to show themselves off as pretty young adults for a night on the town. That left an extra ticket, but John still didn't invite Lou. His chest tightened again, nearly constricting his breathing. Excluded once more. Curse that Paine!

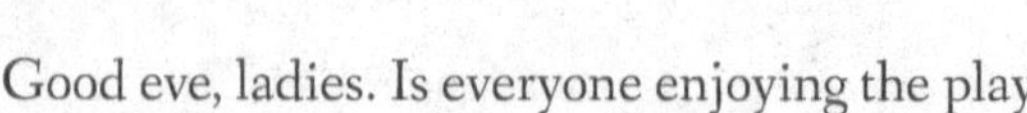

"Good eve, ladies. Is everyone enjoying the play?"

Honora Fitzpatrick turned to see the dashing

John Wilkes Booth, his smile so flashy, she probably could have read her program by its pure white glow. "Mr. Booth!" she greeted him, stifling a giggle.

"Miss Fitzpatrick, so good to see you. And Miss Dean, isn't it? You are looking positively ravishing tonight. Both of you. Truly the belles of the entire theater." He looked over their heads. "Hello, John. Could you and your friend step out? Excuse us, please, ladies. Go right on watching the play. We shan't be long. Business before pleasure, you know."

Booth bowed and flourished his hat as he stepped out into the hall, his raven hair flowing with the movement of his head. He closed the box door on his adoring admirers and turned to John. "Well, whom have we here?"

"Louis Powell, this is our leader, the famous tragedian, John Wilkes Booth. Booth, this is our man from Richmond, Private Louis Powell, late of Mosby's command."

"Good to meet you, Powell." They shook. "I like the grasp of your handshake. Firm, but not too tight, perfect control. That says a lot about a man."

"Hey, Cap, since we'll be working together, you can call me 'Mosby,' if you please." Powell's leering grin revealed his mottled tobacco-stained teeth.

"All right, *Mosby*, you're aware why you're here— to grab Lincoln. John was impressed with your strength. We need a fearless man with your combat experience." Booth stepped back and looked up into Powell's eyes. The hulk towered over him. "Not that we wish to *hurt* Lincoln, but courage is often lacking with stay-at-home types."

"John here says I'm to hold the old man down

until you restrain him with irons." Powell flexed his biceps, leaving no doubt he could do the job.

"More or less." Booth nodded with approval. "I will want you both to come over to Gautier's Oyster House after the play. Everyone will receive his role there. You know where that is, John. Take the young ladies home by cab and come on over as quickly as possible. Say, John, could you pick up a deck of playing cards? It will keep the fast eaters occupied while the rest of us savor the evening's repast. Well, gentlemen, I shall see you shortly after the play. Here's cab fare." He held out a few bank notes.

John started to refuse.

"No, no, I insist." Booth donned his fashionable black slouch hat and saluted the men with a flourish of his shiny walking stick. He then departed and closed the door to the common seats of the dress circle behind him.

John and Powell returned to the play. As they entered the box, John pointed out the broken hasp on the door to the box. "The door will stay shut, but it can't be locked. Ah, this old place." John observed the tattered upholstery stretched across the chairs, the shabby drapes, the carpet worn nearly threadbare. "The whole house needs renovation. But word has it Ford is struggling. He don't take in much, unless Booth feels like playing here."

An hour later, John and Powell alighted from the cab in front of Gautier's on Pennsylvania Avenue, but on the south side of the street. A porter ushered them into the back meeting room to a buffet spread with oysters, cheese and crackers, pate, olives, an array of rare brandy bottles, and fine segars.

"Hey, there they are!" Booth came up and shook

hands. "Let me introduce the rest of the party. Those two huddled together over a noble brandy are Sam Arnold and Mike O'Laughlin, former Confederate soldiers and acquaintances from my boyhood. This youth is Davy Herold, noted partridge shooter, knowledgeable guide, and authority on the roads of Southern Maryland. The man who keeps his own whiskey bottle is George Atzerodt, better known as Port Tobacco. That's where he hails from, and he knows the Potomac crossings like most of us know our own streets." He gestured at Powell with fanfare, as if introducing an actor on the stage, "This is Lewis Powell. You all know John and me. Now, eat and drink up, everyone! There are segars and liquors to appease the most discriminating tastes."

The cohorts gathered around the serving tables as Booth dismissed the waiters with a hefty tip and a jovial, "We will take care of everything, boys!"

They sat and gabbed for almost two hours, full and well-lubricated by then. The room fogged up with segar smoke as they kicked back in their chairs and waited for Booth to take charge of the serious part of the meeting.

"Well, gentlemen, I hope the evening's spread has suited you, one and all!" The actor's voice boomed throughout the room.

He bowed gracefully as Atzerodt and Herold led the cheering and applause. Like all actors and politicians, Booth loved kudos, any time, anywhere. He held up a hand, indicating he wished to get on with business.

"By now, you all know that we're here to plan the abduction of Abraham Lincoln. I need not justify this action to any of you. We have all, in one way or another, aided the South in her noble attempt to secure her freedom in the face of a most powerful Yankee onslaught, be it on the field of battle or through the blockade." He paused for effect. "What I propose to you now is to abduct Lincoln from a theater performance—right in front of God and everybody." The men began to murmur. Booth held up his hand again, the other occupied with segar and brandy snifter. "Please, gentlemen, hear me out entirely. There will be time for questions and comments later. I, naturally, will have the starring role. Along with Powell, who, you may have observed, is as strong as the proverbial ox, I will seize and truss up Lincoln, whether he be in attendance in the lower or upper box." He nodded at O'Laughlin and Herold. "Mike and Davy will shut off the theater gas at the main meter." He turned to Sam Arnold. "Sam will receive the secured president on stage, where, joined by us, daringly and dramatically jumping from the box and covered by the drawn pistols of Mike and Davy, we will spirit him to an awaiting carriage at the back door." He grabbed his left lapel with his free hand. "We will cross the Eastern Branch, probably at Benning's Bridge, which is lightly guarded or often not guarded at all, to meet John Surratt and George Atzerodt who, along with Davy, will pilot us to and across the Potomac. The boats are already purchased and in place on the Port Tobacco inlet. To prevent pursuit, we will tie ropes across the roads, tripping up the galloping Federal cavalry."

He paused once more, a bit longer this time, and stared everyone down. "Any questions so far?" After a beat, he continued, "Once across the river, we will have safe houses and changes of horses all the way to

Richmond. Should we be unable for any reason to move as quickly as I foresee us doing, I have placed extra horses at safe places with provisions, guns, and ammunition at key points along the way. Indeed, I might add, one safe house is within spitting distance of the presidential mansion itself. Now, my good men, have at it!"

John, trying to read the expressions of his co-conspirators, wondered if Booth really expected anyone to speak up and tell him the truth—that his plans were designed to go off half-cocked as they always had. In a theater? That was like charging into the lion's den, and with no Daniel, no Lord God to save them. *Why not just abduct Lincoln on friendly ground?* he wanted to ask their intrepid leader, but Booth was determined to have his audience. John wondered if he could function without one.

But John couldn't keep quiet about Lou. "What about Weichmann?" John spoke up. "He's really miffed about not being given a part."

"He can neither ride nor shoot; you know it, and he knows it," Booth snapped.

"Can we use him for anything?" John persisted. "He keeps hounding me and I'd rather give him some donkey work than risk his ratting us out."

Booth released an impatient hiss through his teeth. "Then tell him we need his expertise in the War Department, getting information on numbers of prisoners held in the North, the secret passwords used at the bridges after dark, that sort of thing. But limit what he knows."

"All well and good..." John's tone carried relief, tinged with an edge of doubt. "But we can't put him off forever without him getting huffed. He already knows too much and could turn against us. If he hasn't already."

"To hell with him." Booth puffed on his segar. "If he's already tattled, I'd have heard about it. He won't open his gob. He's just full of wind and piss." Booth's breath emerged in puffs of smoke.

Those who knew Weichmann laughed heartily in agreement.

Now the actor turned to Arnold and O'Laughlin. Everyone grew silent. "What think you, Sam?"

He stood to his full height and looked Booth square in the eye. "You want to know what I think?" Arnold began. "I think this whole scheme is nuttier than a fruitcake."

Herold and Atzerodt voiced semi-drunken objection.

"Wait, wait." Booth held out his hand. "Let him go on."

"Let us be honest and open about this." Arnold looked around, making eye contact with each of them. "The whole thing is utterly impracticable. First of all, as the purpose of the plan was presented to me, the president was to be captured and taken to Richmond to exchange for our boys in northern prisons. But the exchange has been reopened. So there's no logical purpose to it, unless we act for notoriety alone. I joined for patriotism, not ambition." He looked down, shuffled his feet and seemed reluctant to go on. "Secondly..." his voice cracked, "to do this in a theater full of men, some of whom might be armed, is asking for trouble. All it would take is one man of courage to get up on that stage to delay us long enough for someone else to run out and fetch the police or the provost marshal. They'd be on us like a duck on a June bug. In any plan, I want a shadow of a chance for my life, and I intend to have it in this one."

Lips stayed sealed, all eyes on him.

"Thirdly," he went on, "you tried this already, and Lincoln never showed up." His tone gained confidence. "We should do it some afternoon north of the city as Lincoln goes out on one of his innumerable carriage rides. Hell, in a few weeks he will *live* there for the summer and we can do it almost any day. You *know* Lincoln has dispensed with his cavalry escort. Was too noisy and garish for the rail splitter and his shrew. The road to and from there is perfect. Then, he would be there, guaranteed, and *he* would provide the carriage."

The men snickered at the irony of the Federal government providing the vehicle to accomplish their goal. Booth did not. He stared at Arnold with venomous eyes—eyes that had caused women to swoon and men to draw back in fright when he portrayed Richard the Third. But Arnold never flinched.

"What *you* fail to perceive, Sammy," Booth argued in a far-too-condescending tone, "is that the capture of Lincoln has little to do with the reopening of prisoner exchange. The exchange is more or less a one-to-one process, emphasizing the sick and invalid. What I propose to do is retrieve *all* Southern prisoners held in the North, all at one time, for *one* man: Lincoln. Besides, there are other more important considerations here."

"That merely answers *one* of my objections, and raises more questions about other more important considerations," Arnold insisted. "We have a right to know what we are putting our lives and our families' reputations on the line for. Besides, this has been so wet a spring, I doubt that a carriage could make it all the way to the big river without foundering somewhere. Then what?"

John surmised that Booth resented all this questioning and the possible abandonment of his plan. He had thrown open the floor, naturally expecting no one to have the gall to challenge his convoluted mission. He did not want an open interchange of views. Not like this.

Booth began to bluster. He banged the table with his fist. "Do you know you're liable to be shot?" he shouted at Arnold. "Your oath! You cannot out-run a bullet, Sam!"

But Arnold gamely stood his ground. "By God! Two can play at *that* game, Booth!"

The table emptied, O'Laughlin backing up his comrade, the others siding with Booth. But Powell stayed seated.

John stood and held his hands up in an appeasing gesture. "Now, wait a minute, Booth. What bothers me is that the Yankees are building stockades at the Navy Yard Bridge. The gates open to the South, not to the North as they normally would. As if they were expecting trouble on the city side, within the city, not from the Confederacy. Maybe Arnold is right and we ought to throw up the whole project."

"Well, gentlemen..." Booth drew up to his full height. "If the worse comes to worst, *I* know what to do." He left the obvious unsaid, hanging in the air.

"That does it," Arnold growled. "If I understand you to intimate anything more than the capture of Mr. Lincoln, I, for one, bid you good bye. I am through with this mess! I will have nothing more to do with it. C'mon, Mike."

Arnold and O'Laughlin clapped their hats on their heads. Now realizing the horror of Booth's intention to actually kill Lincoln, John stood, ready to walk out, too.

"Please, gentlemen, your pardon!" Booth intoned with a persuasive air that halted them all in their tracks. "I confess I've had too much champagne. Take my hand in friendship and commonness of purpose. Perhaps we can find something other than the theater approach."

"That's more like it." John heartily shook Booth's outstretched hand.

"There are at least two possibilities, maybe even more," Booth spoke low for dramatic effect. "Lincoln is of the habit of visiting the War Department evenings, usually after dark. He walks over unaccompanied by anyone. We could wait in nearby shrubbery, swarm over him before he knows what has happened, bind and gag him, and take him to a waiting carriage. Then we are off to old Virginia via the Navy Yard Bridge, or maybe the Chain Bridge beyond Georgetown."

"You cannot cross either of those bridges with Lincoln in tow," John corrected him. "Nor the Long Bridge. The guard is way too strong. The only hope would be Benning's Bridge, which is way off to the east. And they're building a stockade there, too. Too risky."

"I have contacts with the Green family who lives in the Van Ness House at the water's edge on Seventeenth Street," Booth countered with braggadocio. "That place is like a fortress out of the Middle Ages. Walls thick as the Tower of London. It's full of secret passages, and deep inside its basement is a trap door to a hidden vault. We can store Lincoln there for a while. Then, when it's safe to move, we ferry him across the Potomac."

"Hold yer horses." Arnold held up his hands. "That presents the same problem of just throwing him in a carriage and leaving the same night. We would never make it across the closest bridges. It's right on the river. I bet those basement rooms are flooded half the time. We'd not only give Lincoln consumption, we'd suffer, too."

"Besides, Booth," John added, "the Greens are among the first the provost marshals will arrest. They're being watched all the time. You know that."

"Oh, hell's teeth!" Booth huffed. "Then we'll try for him on the road to the Old Soldier's Home. It's lonely out there. Not much risk or style in *that*, I daresay. But we must do it soon, or others might beat us to it. And we cannot wait until Lincoln moves there for the summer—that's too late!"

They all stood waiting for his next move.

"Let's sit and play a few hands." Booth pulled up a chair. "There are enough for a rousing poker game, I believe. John, did you bring the cards?"

Shouts of agreement and relief circled the room, as all crowded around Booth. But Arnold and O'Laughlin bowed out and left for their hotel. John joined in the card game, but his mind wandered. Would Lincoln somehow get out to the Old Soldiers' Home before Arnold and O'Laughlin gave it up? Could Powell and Booth subdue Lincoln? Would the bridges be open? Would one man with fortitude stand at the Benning's Bridge stockade and frustrate the whole operation? As he played his hand, he steeled himself silently, *trust to luck. And fate.*

"C'mon! Your raise, Surratt!" Booth's impatient summons jolted him back to reality. At the end of the game, he'd lost every penny. But more was at stake in real life. It gave him a new perspective—and a new maturity.

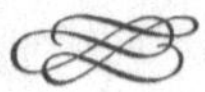

As the hall clock struck ten, Lou heard the pattering of young footsteps on the outside stairway. The girls burst into the parlor in an excited rush, tittering and giggling.

"We got to ride in a taxi home!" Honora yelped. "I need to take the pack of playing cards out to John. Him and Mr. Powell are going out for an after-theater oyster shuck."

Lou tossed his book aside, rose from the chair, and quit the parlor. The joyous atmosphere didn't lift his spirits. His feelings hurt, wishing John had invited him to that oyster shuck, he headed to the kitchen for something warm and filling to eat. *Why do they always leave me out?* he groused as he entered the empty kitchen. He opened the breadbox and tore off a hunk of rye bread. Stuffing it into his mouth, he searched the pantry for some sweets. Not finding any leftover pastries or cakes, he spotted a teacup with a bit of sugar stuck to the bottom, scooped the sugar out and licked it from his fingers.

In the dead of the moonless night, John and Booth rode up Seventh Street to a roadside restaurant at the base of a small rise. Covered by woods, surrounded by dark deathly quiet, it welcomed them with warm lighted windows. "You did pick a perfect place for an ambush," John admitted to Booth. They turned their horses toward the hitching rack that already held four steeds.

"Looks like everyone is here." John dismounted and hitched his horse's reins to the post. A spark of excitement made his heart trip.

Booth slid off his mount. "We may as well go in and get out of the damp."

John peered through a window. Lewis Powell and George Atzerodt sat at a table with Mike O'Laughlin and Sam Arnold. "Hey, Arnold and O'Laughlin are here, how 'bout that. I thought they'd reached the end of their rope with this whole thing."

"I made peace with them, even though it galled me. But they'll be useful, so I had to eat humble pie. Sometimes you have to make sacrifices for the dear old South." Booth nudged past John and opened the door.

Asking two friends to reconsider a plot to kidnap the president is what he reckons to be a sacrifice for the South? John needed to show Booth some of Mathew Brady's photos of dead soldiers scattered across battle-fields and tell the misinformed actor about *real* sacrifice.

Booth and John ordered brandies and joined the others at their table.

"Sam was awondering if you really said to meet here at two o'clock," O'Laughlin remarked with a grin.

"Hrumph!" Arnold grunted.

"I would not have gotten us horses and guns just to leave y'all hanging." Booth pulled up a chair. "We were held up by the muddy roads."

"Yeah, as I told Sam, 'don't be alarmed—he'll show,'" O'Laughlin said. "It *was* looking bad. Rain all day but clearing now."

"Well, gentlemen, shall we review our roles?" Booth asked as each tossed back a mouthful of whiskey. "I already sent Davy down to Tee Bee, to set up the escape route. Joe Huntt secretly keeps extra horses. Davy also has ropes to tie across the road to confuse pursuing cavalry, wrenches to remove the wheels from Lincoln's coach for the river crossing on the barge, and extra guns and ammunition. I got another actor, John Mathews, to ship provisions to Dr. Mudd's. George Atzerodt has a couple of barges laid hidden in Goose Bay for crossing Lincoln and his dismantled coach over the Potomac." Booth snapped his fingers and held out his empty glass. A server refilled it.

He went on, "Sam and Mike will ride out ahead and flank the horses of the coach. Just let it catch up to you, boys. When it does, pull aside, each to the opposite side of the road, and close on the team quickly, pulling it down."

He turned to John. "You and George take care of the coachman. Do not fire a shot unless you must. Just club him and take possession of the driver's seat. Drive into Maryland by way of Benning's Bridge. George will pick up the loose horses and follow, you other two riding post."

Booth's fiery eyes pierced all of them, one at a

time. "Lewis and I will take care of the old baboon. "I trust you got the ropes and handcuffs, Lewis?"

"That I did, Cap." He nodded.

"Splendid. Now, you all enjoy life here for a while. Go slow on the liquor, y'hear? I don't need a gang of drunks who can't ride upright or shoot straight. I'm going up to the hospital and see where they are in the performance. Then I'll return and we can go out on the road just ahead of Lincoln. No need to hang around outside where some passerby might get curious or alarmed."

Booth excused himself and exited.

John checked his pocket watch every fifteen minutes or so. As the time dragged on, he and the others began to get fidgety. They'd exhausted several topics —the weather, horses, who made the best whiskey. After an hour of trading war stories, there was nothing else for them to do. John thought of asking the men if they wanted to sing a few songs, but the mood just didn't seem right.

After a stretch that seemed like another hour, John checked his watch. Only ten minutes had dragged by. "How long has Booth been gone?" Arnold asked for what seemed like the tenth time.

O'Laughlin pulled out his pocket watch and popped the cover. "About an hour or so. I... look!" He rose to a semi-standing position and pointed out the window. "There he is now. Coming up the road lickety split!"

"Christ Almighty!" Powell swore. "At that pace, he's gonna wear that danged beast out right before we need him."

Booth stormed through the door, face contorted in

rage, slouch hat askew, blackened boots spattered with mud.

"Damn it to hell!" Booth reached the table, swept off his hat and flung it to the floor. The bartender and servers looked his way. "Lincoln is not there!" His voice lowered to a harsh whisper. "The son of a bitch never showed up! I saw Davenport. He said the old man had sent his regrets. Pressing business elsewhere. Pressing business, *elsewhere?* Doesn't he know that his most *pressing* business is *here?*"

"Scheiss!" Atzerodt pumped his fist in the air.

John summed up the whole matter in a phrase, "Oh, what a hot mess."

All the men griped except Powell. He just sat there, calm as ever, awaiting orders. But a frown contorted his features. "What now, Cap?" he asked as the hub-bub died out.

"Let's not panic." Booth paced to and fro. "We don't need to pile out of here all at once. Go out in twos and threes, just like we came in."

"This is it, Booth." Arnold headed for the door. "Mike and I are through. You can find our horses at that stable back of the National Hotel—Phumphries I guess they call it. We're going back to Baltimore. Permanently."

"Wait up." Powell stood. "I'll ride back with y'all."

"Booth," John suggested, "what's say we ride north a couple of miles and then head back into the city?"

Booth rubbed his eyes, looking exhausted. "Good idea. It'll put some distance between us and them."

"Tomorrow, you and the Sauerkraut take my horses and ride out and fetch in Davy. Can you hide the weapons and ropes somewhere?" Booth asked.

"Yeah." John nodded. "In the roadhouse at Surrattsville."

As John and Booth departed, they looked over at Atzerodt. He drained his drink and sidled up to the bar for another.

"Let him stay here and get squiffed," Booth said. "There's not a damn thing else for him to do now."

What could any of us do now? John wondered.

CHAPTER 10

Lou HID his disappointment when Mrs. Surratt didn't appear at the dinner table the next evening. Amidst a bland discussion about the weather, Annah banged her knife upon the table. Lou nearly jumped out of his skin and dropped his fork with clang against his plate piled with roast chicken and boiled potatoes. "Miss Surratt, what is the matter?"

"Mr. Weichmann, if anything were to happen to my brother John through his acquaintance with Booth I would kill him!" Her voice, shrill and loud, would have shattered glass if she'd continued her rampage.

"Him? You do mean Booth, I hope." Lou picked up his fork and piled more potatoes onto it, now used to the sudden emotional outbursts common around this house.

"Of course!" She flung down her serviette, scraped her chair back, stood and fled the dining room, leaving Lou to shrug and shake his head at a now nearly empty table.

He peered over at her full pate. "She hardly touched a bite. Waste not want not." He proceeded to scrape her leavings onto his own plate and devoured the meal as Miss Fitzpatrick pushed her plate away.

"You can have mine, too, Mr. Weichmann." She craned her neck to see into the kitchen. "I wonder what's for dessert."

His belly full after the generous dinner, Lou entered the hall and bumped into Mrs. Surratt, not looking where she was going, weeping bitterly.

He halted in his tracks. "Mrs. Surratt, what is it? What happened?"

"Mr. Weichmann, John is gone away! John is gone away!" She swiped at her tears with a handkerchief and pushed past him out of his sight.

He stood there staring at the wall, baffled. *John is gone away? He goes away all the time.*

Shaking his head, knowing he'd find out sooner or later, he went upstairs and lay down on his bed to read *The Pickwick Papers*. As he lost himself in his novel, John pounded up the stairs and burst into their room. Looking up, to his astonishment Lou noticed John's pantaloons were stuffed into his muddy boot tops. He drew a four-barreled Sharps revolver, made for concealing in men's waistcoats or ladies' purses, from his vest pocket. With a wild-eyed look, he leveled it at Lou.

"What's the matter, John?" He didn't take it as a good-natured joke. "For the love of Pete, put that thing down!" Lou cowered and sidled over to the edge of the bed. "That's the number one rule of our local militia, never point guns at people!"

"How can we win the war, then?" John lowered the gun and shoved it into his waistband. "My prospects are gone, my hopes blasted." His voice cracked with fatigue as he hung his head in a gesture of defeat.

"What happened?" Lou held his place in the book with his forefinger.

Without answering Lou's question, John sat next to him. "Can you get me a clerkship? I want something to do."

Lou blinked in astonishment. "You—asking *me* for something to do?" After all Lou's pleading and wheedling? "Oh, you foolish fellow! Why don't you settle down and be contented? I swear, I do not understand you lately, since your acquaintance with that actor. What in Sam Hill is going on?"

John still didn't answer him. He just sat there, head in hands, shoulders slumped. Lou placed a comforting hand on John's shoulder.

Footsteps clomped up the stairs, and there stood Powell, every inch the brigand, face flushed, from drink, Lou reckoned, though he stood in a soldier's erect posture. His wrinkled and torn clothes caked with mud, he wore spurs of the cavalry style. Upon spotting Lou he stopped to fasten one of his suspenders.

Powell brushed back his shabby coat and pulled up his waistcoat, as if fastening a suspender, and revealed a six-shooter stuffed in a holster resting on his hip. More footsteps, and John Wilkes Booth sauntered in. Dressed in dark tailored velvet jacket and trousers, black slouch hat with rim turned down, white kid gloves, he filled the room with his commanding presence. Nobody spoke as Booth circled the room, rhythmically slapping the side of his spit-shined boot with a gold-handled riding crop.

Lou didn't see any firearms on him. "H-hello, Booth." He finally got up the nerve to speak.

Booth halted and looked at him as if he couldn't remember where he'd met hm. "Why, you here! I didn't see you."

Booth gave a signal to the others, and one by one they clomped upstairs to the attic. Lou knew he ought not follow, although he had a hankering to know what these hoodlums were cooking up. A while later, the pounding started on the stairs again. This time it continued all the way down to the second-story landing, outside and down the porch steps. None of the men spoke as they passed Lou, still on his bed, reading his *Pickwick Papers*—or, pretending to.

What in tarnation is going on in this house? Unnerved by tonight's unsound behavior in this house, Lou grappled with the question as he did more and more lately. Why were John and Booth so chummy all of a sudden? Up to now, he hadn't regarded their sudden and extraordinary friendship in a serious light. Booth was not acting and had no visible employment, nor did John. Was it boredom? What was at the bottom of it all? He didn't pay much attention to Atzerodt's frequent visits to the house. When Booth came over, they would all file into a room—occasionally with Mrs. Surratt in attendance—and shut the door. Herold came once or twice in mid-March, when Powell was boarding.

To the extent that Lou could snoop or eavesdrop, he could not get to the bottom of these proceedings. But the mysterious language and phrases John and Mrs. Surratt sometimes dropped, the meanings of which Lou was too naïve to interpret, aroused his worst suspicions. Something unlawful—perhaps criminal—was going on in this house.

That night he decided to take the plunge and report these suspicious goings-on. But upon awakening in the dead of night, drenched in cold sweat, he thought again. The next day he kept his mouth clamped shut.

~

The next morning, John and Atzerodt grabbed a couple of Booth's horses from Howard's Stable. The pair thundered across the Navy Yard Bridge and stopped at Surrattsville to see if Herold was there. Not finding him, they listened to bartender John Lloyd—still smarting from a drubbing Herold gave him at cards—complain of Herold laughing merrily each time he won a hand.

With a few shots of whiskey in them, John and Atzerodt spurred their horses out of Surrattsville. A mile or so down the road, John spotted Herold lumbering up, his buggy bristling with weapons and ropes.

"Where in holy hell you been?" Herold shouted as they came up. "How'd it go? Where's Lincoln? Where's Booth and the others?"

"Aw!" John drew up to Herold. "It all went straight down the potty."

"How'z'at?"

"We never saw Lincoln. He was somewhere else —at Booth's hotel, the National, in fact. Can you beat that? We would have been better off if we just stayed in town. But there was too many people around the National to have done anything."

"Ja!" Atzerodt confirmed in German, "Ganz Un-sinn! Schrecklich!"

"Talk English, George," John admonished. Only Lou could speak to the German émigré in his own tongue.

Herold shook his head. "Now what? Both Thompson and Huntt down at Tee Bee will have nothing to do with the guns. I asked."

"Take everything back to Ma's tavern," John instructed. "Lloyd can hide it for us. We just come through there anyways."

The trio entered the loud crowded tavern, the air thick with smoke. Lloyd sprinted back and forth behind the bar serving customers.

"Let's just sit, drink, and play cards until the crowd thins out," John suggested. He got no argument from Atzerodt and Herold.

During a break in the flow of patrons, John commented, "I've never seen so many in the morning." But it was Saturday, and folks usually stopped to fortify themselves against the cold trip to Washington.

"Come in here, Mr. Lloyd." John pulled Lloyd into the front parlor, off limits to the public.

"What's all that mess?" Lloyd pointed to the Spencer carbines, box of cartridges, pile of rope, and monkey wrench on the front room sofa.

John shut the door. "Just a few items that I want you to hide for us for a little while."

"What's *a little while?*" Lloyd narrowed his eyes, his tone suspicious.

"Until we need them, whenever that will be."

"I ain't got noplace to hide this crap." He waved John away. "The Feds come by without a moment's notice and case this joint for contraband. I ain't goin'a jail for the likes of you three, I guarantee!"

"Shh! Simmer down!" John held his finger to his lips.

"No way, dammit!" Lloyd turned to leave.

"Wait." John grasped Lloyd's sleeve. "I'll show you a place no one but us will know about. We've hid stuff there for years and it's never been found. Grab a few of those things." John picked up a carbine in its leather case and the monkey wrench.

Lloyd growled assent more than he said it. He grabbed the other Spencer, the length of rope, and the box of cartridges. They went into the former storeroom, now the kitchen, past some kegs of liquor and beer.

"Let's leave the rope and wrench here. No one will suspect them." They put the items on the floor. "Now let's go upstairs."

They ascended the hall stairs and turned into Annah's old room. John slid a chest of drawers away from the south wall and pushed against the lath. A small door, about half the height of a standard one, swung open. The musty attic smell wafted out over the kitchen odors from below. The unfinished room extended over the used portion of the house. The floor joists and wall framing were not covered by lath and plaster, but exposed.

"I hain't never seen this room before!" Lloyd's eyes widened in wonderment as John stepped into the opening.

"I know. Neither have the Yanks." He grinned, winking.

"Coulda used this to put up travelers' slaves, instead of making them sleep out back." Lloyd peered inside. "Dammit, nobody tells me nothin'!"

"Watch me, and put your carbine next to mine." John shoved the weapon and its case between two joists under the floor. Lloyd followed suit. Then the two men returned to the occupied part of the house.

"Reckon we'll play cards for a while and have another drink," John headed back into the tavern.

"I hope you'll come back and take those blasted things away." Lloyd scowled. "They give me the willies."

The next day, as John and Atzerodt went into Southern Maryland to pick up Herold and the weapons, Lou accosted Major Gleason outside his office.

"Major, sir, remember that problem I told you about a couple of weeks ago? The strange goings-on at my boarding house? You were right. Nothing to worry about. Whatever the group had planned seems to have been abandoned. They have dispersed."

"I *told* you it was a silly notion, Weichmann. I daresay we will never hear from them again." He walked out into the hall, Lou at his heels. "Kidnap the president, indeed." He snickered. Several officers passed him and smiled. *Let 'em wonder what's so funny.* Gleason didn't laugh much at work, and when he did, he kept the joke to himself. But he might not keep this joke under his collar for much longer.

John greeted Gustavus Howell at the door to his mother's boarding house and invited him inside. Howell, an ardent Confederate partisan, specialized in running folks, goods, and information through the lines between Richmond and Washington City, and all points North by way of New York City to Montreal.

"Come on in, Gus. You want a whiskey or—"

"I can't stay long, thanks anyway." He didn't even remove his hat. "John, you need to go to New York City to pick up Nettie Slater and escort her to Surrattsville." He lowered his voice and cupped his hand to the side of his mouth. "I am too hot for that sort of thing right now. The Yanks and their agents are keeping too sharp an eye on me, and we don't want to unduly compromise our top female courier."

This top female courier would now be his charge! He genuinely admired Howell, and beamed with pride that the feeling was mutual. Thoughts of Nettie Slater conjured up a well of fantasies for him.

"No one knows much about this mysterious young widow except that she's a fast mover and a crack shot," Howell said.

"Well, I've hungered to meet her ever since I joined The Cause." John couldn't keep the excitement out of his voice as his pulse raced. *Will she like me?* he wondered. Forget protocol and professionalism. He thought solely like a man as he imagined working with the elusive female courier. Even Booth would be green with envy. Oh, he had to tell Cap about this!

"I've heard of Nettie Slater, of course, but have never met her. How will I know her? When will I know to go?" John's words tumbled out.

"Keep your pants on, son," Howell drawled. "You will get a very special telegram from a company in New York called Demille's. Do what it says. It will mean that you are to take the next train to New York and meet the good lady in front of A.T. Stewart's dry goods store on Broadway. He calls it a 'dee-partment store' nowadays. Don't go to the 200 block of Broadway. That's the old dry goods place, now a warehouse. The new dee-partment store is grander than ever. Mrs. Lincoln squanders her husband's presidential salary there, I hear. It's in the 900 block, between Ninth and Tenth."

"How will I know her?" he asked again. "Surely there will be other ladies waiting in front of such a popular place."

"Well, o'course!" Howell playfully poked John in the chest. "But all of these ladies will lack one thing. They will not be holding a horsehair switch in their hands, with the waxed end threaded through her fingers, every other finger on top. You just pick up that gal. You'll find her a most comely, sweet, young thing, although she will cover her face with one o' them thick masque veils, as they call'm."

"No kiddin'? Shucks! After all this, I won't get to see her face? She must be a big target if she has to hide like that." John's voice cracked like a growing boy's.

"Yep. She's a target, all right. In more ways than one. Most men would just love to rove their mitts over her delectable body of an evening, never mind gettin' information outta her. But I hear she's as frigid as a polar bear's tit. Nobody ever got near her. We calls her the French Woman. Travels under a French passport. Speaks the stuff, too, and English without an accent, unless someone suspicious talks to her, then she puts a Frenchy one on. Use the code words 'Come Retribution,' when you greet her. She will answer,

'Complete Victory.' You got that?"

"Got it." He nodded, heart beating an energized tattoo. This was more intriguing than the plot with Booth! A beautiful female spy! A beautiful *French* female spy! If only he could blab this to Lou, but he couldn't let Lou get a crumb of what he was up to now. If he blew this, he'd live the rest of his life as a hermit in disgrace, forever branded the blabbermouth who'd let the South down.

"I'm mighty flattered you trust me with this, Mr. Howell," John thanked him sincerely. "I mean, there are other men more experienced and equipped than me to handle this."

Howell chuckled. "You'd think so. But men being men, I don't trust any of 'em."

John took that as a backhanded compliment. Did Howell think he was a Nancy-boy just because he'd never been seen in the company of a woman? Or was it his association with Lou, who he himself wondered about at times? But Howell continued, "You're the most reliable courier I know in these parts, John. The others would never be able to keep their yip yaps shut about a mission with a beautiful woman. They'd blabber it all over the landscape and we'd be dead meat for certain."

John whistled in relief. Good thing it wasn't for the reason he'd suspected.

"I'll eagerly await the message, Mr. Howell. And just as equally await meeting Mrs. Slater." He extended his hand to shake Howell's.

After Howell left, John grabbed his coat and headed towards Pennsylvania Avenue. Where would Cap be now? Just dying to tell him, John dashed down the street and broke into a sweaty run.

He didn't find Booth, but he knocked back at least two celebratory shots of whiskey in every tavern he hit. When he staggered home, his mother gave him a good tongue-lashing, but she'd see the light on another day. Right now all he wanted to do was sleep it off.

~

"Ma, we need to take turns at the window to look out for a telegram from New York," John told his mother the next day. She didn't probe further, and he didn't volunteer any more information. She just went to the window to relieve him every two hours, sitting there with her knitting and rosary beads. During his turn, he skimmed the papers, looking up after every other paragraph, hardly knowing what he read. He couldn't keep his mind on anything else. Good thing Lou didn't ask any nosy questions; he kept to himself reading his Dickens and going to his drill meetings. At mealtimes, John pushed his food around his plate, too worked up to eat. His mother didn't comment, knowing he was anxious about this telegram, but his sister had at him. "What's with you, Johnny, doesn't my cooking please your palate anymore?"

"No, your vittles are as yummy as ever. I just have a lot on my mind." She remedied that by giving his untouched food to Lou, who devoured it. Nothing went to waste in the Surratt house.

On the third day, as his mother came to the window for her shift, he told her who the telegram would be from and the reason for this mission. "By the bye, I'll be traveling with Mrs. Slater," he added, forcing a casual tone.

Mary patted her son on the arm. "Just be careful,

John. I've heard about that woman. They say she's a Jezebel. If you want to do this, I won't stand in your way, but don't fall into her trap."

"What trap?" He raised his hands, palms up. "It's strictly business."

But the wily grin playing on his mother's lips told him she believed that as much as he did. "John, you're a grown man now. But she happens to be a bit more grown. Need I say more?"

"No, ma. I'm a gentleman. And if she's a lady, there's nothing to worry about."

"I'd feel better if you were chaperoned." She sat in the chair he vacated and wound her rosary beads around her fingers.

"Oh, maaaa!" John threw his arms up and let them fall to his sides.

"All right, all right. But keep one thing firmly in mind." She looked up at him. "I'm too young to be a grandmother."

He turned away so she wouldn't see him blushing to his roots. Why was she always a step ahead of him, all his life?

~

Finally, the missive from New York arrived, as Howell had promised. John almost broke down the door to grab it from the delivery boy's hands. But it was in the form of a letter, not a telegram.

March 19, '65

Mr. John Surratt
    Dear Sir:

I would like to see you on important business if you can spare the time to come to New York.

Please telegraph me immediately on the reception of this whether you can come or not & oblige.

Yours & etc.,

R.D. Watson

P.S. Address care of Demille & Co.

178 1/2 Water St.

R.D. Watson? John thought a moment, stroking his whiskers. Oh, sure! Roderick D. Watson, from Charles County, a noted Confederate contact from his old Secret Mail Line days. He'd spent most of last year at Fort Lafayette in New York Harbor, a guest of the Feds, accused of blockade running. Everyone in Southern Maryland knew R.D. Watson!

He telegraphed his willingness to show.

Before he left for the train station, his mother took him aside. "Listen, son...Gus Howell fears that the Feds are hot to arrest him and anyone associated with him. I share his fears. So when you and Miz Slater get here, you go to the Metropolitan Hotel. I will have rooms reserved for you under the alias 'Henry Sherman.' This will allow you to rest without picking up a Union agent watching our house. They are out there all the time."

Mary parted the parlor curtains to a finger's width and peered out the window. "Nobody out there, but that don't mean nothing—them Federal spies are sneakier'n a fox in July." She turned to face him. "The next morning, you will go around to Howard's Stable in the next square and get ahold of Mr. Stabler, the stable manager. He'll have a two-horse team and conveyance ready. The grays are good animals. Then you drive over and pick up Miz Slater. The two of you come over here. We will have a breakfast ready and be on the road before the Federal agents even get up. They never stay all night. By the way, I'm going with y'all to the tavern. I have some business with Mr. Lloyd and Gus Howell will be there, too. Then you can carry me home and put up the rig and team with Mr. Stabler that evening."

"Got it, Ma." He scribbled his orders in a tiny notepad he kept in his top pocket. "Mr. Stabler? That's a fitting name for a stable manager. I don't gotta write that down."

CHAPTER 11

WHEN JOHN REACHED New York City, he reported to Demille's. All he had time for that night was dinner and a bath. Early the next morning, he strolled up Broadway, gawking at the sites. He'd never seen anything like the bustling metropolis—buildings stood squeezed together in block-long rows or separated by narrow, filthy alleys piled with stinking refuse. Carriages and omnibuses clogged the manure-strewn streets. Grim-faced pedestrians scurried about, heads down, jostling each other out of their paths with umbrellas and jutting elbows. The cool breeze off the Hudson River carried the stench of manure and rotting garbage. Pushcart peddlers hollered their wares and prices, their lopsided wooden carts piled with fruits and vegetables. A network of black telegraph wires crisscrossed above, blocking out all but patches of sky. It made Washington City look like a sleepy hamlet. The frantic colorful scene seemed to rush by at high speed. He got dizzy just standing on the corner watching it all. This pace would take some getting used to.

He crossed Ninth Street and approached Stewart's Department Store's glass revolving doors and full-length windows dressed with the latest fashions. A stunning young woman in a blue dress held a horse-hair switch, alternate fingers on top.

One look at this raven-haired beauty turned John to a quivering mass of sweaty, trembling jelly. Tongue-tied, he sidled up to her. "Uh—c-come Retribution?" he murmured out of the side of his mouth.

"Complete Victory," came the response, her voice warm, sultry, inviting.

"I am John Surratt. Mr. Gus Howell was—"

"Nettie Slater," she cut him off. "You may call me Miz Nettie. Shall we go, *Mr. Surratt*? The less said, the better. Please fetch my satchels." She pointed to a pair of carpetbags on the ground behind her. Obeying her command, he picked them up like a dutiful porter.

They moved off silently in the direction of the Hudson River docks, just in time for the ferry to Jersey City and the Pennsylvania Railroad's subsidiaries headed south. Each line had its own depot. Passengers had to make their way between them on their own.

His attempt at chitchat was painful enough, not being a great conversationalist, especially with women. All they had in common at this point was the war, so he began telling her about his courier activities. He even mentioned Booth, careful not to go into much detail.

But she only nodded or answered "yes" or "no." She sure was serious about "the less said, the better." He finally gave up and dug out Lou's worn copy of *A Tale of Two Cities*.

While waiting for train connections, John took

the opportunity to call on Lewis Powell again. His current cover was as a clerk for Parr's China Halls, a store that sold china. It was also a Confederate drop-off point. The owner, David Parr, an active Confederate agent, transshipped goods and couriers through the Monument City.

While Powell and John spoke outside on the street, Powell's local girlfriend, Mary Branson, took the opportunity to wander through Mr. Parr's store.

She spotted him behind a counter adding up some figures. "Mr. Parr?"

He looked up and smiled. "Yes, Miss Branson."

"Where does he, I mean Mr. Harrison, live?" she asked.

"Why, I think he's from Washington City, my dear."

"And who is that beautiful lady, the one with the masque veil, who came in with him?" she probed further.

"Mrs. Slater." He slid his pencil behind his ear. "She's a very brave lady of French extraction, I believe, who works on the most confidential basis for us."

"Mary! We're ready!" Powell called from the doorway, where John stood with Nettie.

"Good day, Mr. Parr. We're off to dinner down at the railroad station," Mary called over her shoulder. "Thank you for ever'thang."

The two couples parted company on the street and Powell bowed to kiss Nettie's hand. She seemed to relish the attention, making John wonder what he'd been doing wrong for the last twenty-four hours. It wasn't that Powell was any more dashing—John was just a tad shorter and thinner. He made a mental note to kiss her hand at the end of the evening, if he didn't fall all over himself first.

By the time the travelers transferred to the Baltimore and Ohio for the last leg into Washington City, they had yet to utter more than a few words, all related to train movements. He was still Mr. Surratt and she was Miz Nettie, by her professed choice. But her perfume spoke volumes from behind the dark masque veil. The sweet fragrance exuding a hint of lilacs, coupled with his imagination, drove John wild with desires unbefitting a young man once contemplating priesthood.

John and Nettie reached Washington City late that evening. They didn't head for the Surratt townhome, but turned in at the Metropolitan Hotel first as his Ma had instructed.

Even though his mother acting as chaperone did not appeal to John's increasingly prurient thoughts about Nettie, the plan went off without a hitch. Mary saw to it everyone was quiet the next morning, so that Lou would not cotton on. As fortune would have it, John, Mrs. Surratt, and Nettie pulled out from the curb and turned toward the Avenue before Lou even appeared at the table.

~

As the grays pulled the four-seater into the Surratsville tavern's yard, John Lloyd ran out, waving his arms.

"Land sakes," he panted, "it's a good thing you weren't here last night. Federal cavalry broke in and arrested Gus Howell. Yanked him right outta bed."

"It is just like he feared." Mary's voice quivered.

"Good thing they didn't pass by us on the way here. They could have bagged us all. That would have been a real coup for that dastardly Lafayette Baker!"

"But there is no one to drive Miz Slater to the river and squire her to Richmond." Lloyd caught his breath. "What'll we do now?"

"John will have to do it." Mary turned to her son. "You can escort her all the way through to Richmond, son. It's the only way. Go over to the Barry house and ask Mr. Barry to accompany you to the river. He can bring the rig back to Mr. Stabler. I will pick up the stage from Leonardtown later today to return to the city thataway."

John's heart leapt for joy at the thought of taking Nettie to Richmond, but crumbled when he realized that Mr. Barry would tag along as an un-wanted chaperone. His mother was a step ahead of him all the way. She already knew he was "smitten," as she warned him earlier, but feared the worldly and widowed *femme fatale* was far too sophisticated for him.

When John, Nettie, and David Barry reached Port Tobacco, John sent Barry back to Washington City with the team, the rig, and a letter for Stabler:

Mr. Brooke:

As business will detain me for a few days in the country, I thought I would send you your team back. Mr. Barry will deliver it safety and pay the hire on it. If Mr. Booth, my friend, should want my horses, let him have them, but no one else. If you should want any money on them, he will let you have it. I should like to have the team for several days, but it is too expensive, especially as I have

women on the brain, and may be away a week
or two.

Yours respectfully,
J. Harrison Surratt

With that final stab at Brooke Stabler for teasing him, John vowed that somehow he and the Jezebel would rectify all those lost moments. After all, she *was* French.

~

In a Confederacy full of English-speaking Scots-Irish, George Atzerodt's name presented a puzzle. When he introduced himself in his thick German-accented English, the universal response was, "Huh?" So everyone who frequented the Secret Mail Line just referred to him by his moniker, "Port Tobacco," the name of his home town. No one knew who had originated it, but it fit.

Most, like Mary Surratt, saw George Atzerodt as a drunken nobody. Atzerodt was content to leave it at that. It kept people from prying into his affairs. They assumed that he had none worth knowing about. But he was far from an inconsequential, nondescript lush. He was an expert boatman, stealthily running the Yankee blockade on the Potomac.

"Die Potomac cross I like a shpook," he liked to chuckle in his broken English filled with inverted German grammar. "I goes mittin a qavater mile off die Yankees und dere double-enders."

John looked at Nettie and shrugged. The half-dozen other men murmured among themselves. They did not have John's instinctive trust of Atzerodt's river-negotiating talents. Most of them had never run the blockade over the water, preferring landed routes.

Atzerodt ignored the grousing and assigned the men to sit side by side, with four rowers sitting midships. Atzerodt picked John as one of them. The other three were husky, hard-muscled youths. He sat Nettie in the bow, and another man in the stern, where Atzerodt would handle the tiller. The other two sat with the rowers, pistols drawn against possible Yankee interference.

"Ven I say dick..."

"That means dig," John muttered to his seatmate.

"...you row zusammen—uh, togetter," Atzerodt commanded. "Ven I say shtop, you halten."

The rowers commenced, falling into rhythm, as Atzerodt guided them out on the river in the fading daylight. He headed their craft straight toward Lt. Charles Cawood's Confederate signal camp on the Virginia shore opposite Port Tobacco. Out on the water, a Union double-ender chugged up the river, its paddle wheels splashing and churning against the current of dark water ebbing out to sea.

The rowers strained and sweated at their work. Just as they left the main channel and pulled into the Virginia shallows, a gruff voice commanded, "Heave to and stand by to be boarded! Surrender or you will be fired upon!"

"Shtop!" Atzerodt commanded the rowers. "Ve surrender!" He stood, arms upraised.

The four rowers shipped their oars and the boat drifted with the tide. In the gathering darkness, a Yankee gunboat appeared out of nowhere. A longboat full of armed sailors and marines floated at its side.

The sailors manned their oars and pulled alongside Atzerodt's craft.

"Get ready those of you with pistols!" Nettie ordered from the bow. "Shoot on my command when they come close."

The French woman reached into her reticule and brought forth a short-barreled Colt's pocket pistol. The man beside her drew a Remington six-shooter from his belt. The man next to Atzerodt in the stern held a cocked Colt's Navy revolver.

"What the hell is she gonna do? Shake hands with them?" One of the rowers next to John growled disgustedly as the Union longboat pulled alongside them.

"Fire!" Nettie's soprano command echoed through the dusk. She pulled the trigger. The whole river seemed to explode. Birds screeched and screamed. Feathers fluttered through the air. As Confederate fire found its mark, several marines wailed in agony.

"Dick! Dick hardt!" Atzerodt shrieked above the din.

The fugitives' boat shot ahead as the four men's oars hit the water at the same moment. Atzerodt guided them into the shallows. Confusion buzzed in the Yankee boat as the Confederate fusillade cut down the coxswain, their boat commander, and many more. A few stray bullets sang around the fugitive craft as falling bodies and continued hostile fire upset other gunmen's aims. But no one was hit—no pursuit from the Federals. The gunboat held its cannon fire for fear of accidentally hitting its own men.

"Mein Gott!" Atzerodt prayed as they ran the boat into the river bank. "Dat vas close!"

"Too close," John intoned to no one in particular. He staggered onto shore, exhausted. The men in the boat slumped and breathed hard.

Lt. Cawood came running up, pistol at the ready. "Are all y'all safe?"

Everyone checked their clothes for bullet holes and felt for damp blood. "We-all are fine," came the reply in concert.

John collapsed on a patch of grass and sprawled out on his back. He turned his head and breathed in the mossy aroma of earth. Oh, to be on terra firma again! He flung an arm over his eyes as the recent events ran through his mind at top speed. He could honestly say this was the closest he'd ever come to death. Was it worth it? The Cause was his life's mission, but he wouldn't be doing it any good as a corpse. He wanted to stay alive and fulfill his quest here on Earth, to help win this war and gain the South the independence she needed and deserved.

A vivid image of his father's face flashed before his mind's eye. Disillusioned when he was mature enough to realize the old man's shortcomings and faults, he still held a place in his heart for Pa; he'd made time for John during the most important moments of his childhood. Now he wanted to prove his bravery to Pa, to carry on the Surratt name with pride. He opened his eyes and gazed into the heavens. "I'm doing this for you, dear Pa, for you and for the South, in that order."

So, treacherous as it was out here, he couldn't quit now. He'd never forgive himself. And he'd never let his Pa down. He would've done the same thing, given the opportunity.

John knew he'd been put here in this time and

place for a reason. He'd never be as famous as Booth or Robert E. Lee, but he'd make at least some history books. It would happen, he just knew it.

After a sleepless night at Cawood's camp, the party set off for the Richmond, Fredericksburg and Potomac Railroad by horseback and army ambulance, leaving Atzerodt behind. They traveled all day and reached the rails at Guiney's Station near Fredericksburg. Here they encamped with a Virginia regiment returning from a winter furlough, on its way to the Richmond trenches. Several officers and men took John and Nettie on a tour of the area.

"There's the house old Stonewall died in." One of the officers pointed to a small building of weather-beaten gray clapboards. "See that window? He drew his last breath in that bedroom. 'Let us cross the river and rest under the shade of the trees.' Those were his last words, so I read." His voice broke with emotion.

Everyone stood in rapt silence for a moment to honor the man General Robert E. Lee eulogized as "his right arm." John bowed his head as a sudden rush of grief bathed his eyes in tears.

They moved off to a nearby apple orchard to rest. As they sat enjoying the calm evening, sipping coffee and munching apples, a faint clicking noise sounded nearby. "What's that?" John's eyes darted around.

"Shh! That's a telegraphic key," a soldier replied. "Damn! It's to some headquarters—and I don't reckon it's ours."

The party hurried to regimental headquarters and reported their suspicions to the officer in charge. He called the regimental colonel, who ordered an armed patrol to investigate. John went along. Nettie insisted on joining them, over the objections of several officers. "A woman has no place in such an expedition," one of them snarled.

"I have been shot at before, sir, in fact, just the other night," she snapped, shutting him right up.

John and the others from the river crossing vouched for Nettie's gutsy action in the fight with the Union gunboat. The patrol crept up to the house at the orchard, bayoneted rifles at the ready. Nettie leveled her pistol. John kept his in his belt, harboring a queasy feeling that this was going to be a long night of violence, blood, and gore—and inevitably, death.

As his men surrounded the house, the lieutenant and a couple of soldiers broke down the door. Inside, they found the telegrapher cowering in a garret closet, telegraphic key at his side. They trussed him up and dragged him to headquarters.

"Look what we found! A damned Yankee spy! Let's hang him! String him up!" The condemning taunts pierced the night air.

"You can't do that!" John insisted. "He's in uniform. He must be made a prisoner of war."

"Aw, c'mon, Colonel Moore," the men goaded. "Let's stretch his neck!"

To John's horror, the colonel submitted to popular demand. With Nettie leading the cheering regiment, soldiers produced rope and hauled up the doomed Yankee soldier by his neck to die—without benefit of a drop. He slowly strangled to death, gagging and thrashing.

"Woo-ee! Lookit 'im dance." One soldier pointed and laughed.

"See his eyes bug out," chirped another.

"You can hear 'im gag!" A sergeant guffawed.

John could not bear to watch. He turned, staggered into the woods, and retched. He didn't rejoin the group—he needed some time alone. How could war produce such savage reactions in the human heart? And what of their souls? His mind raced back to his school days, that time of lost innocence not so long ago.

Oh, what was it Sir Walter Scott wrote? It was in *Marmion*, that piece where the fortunes of Scottish Lord Marmion are shown in association with the castle, the convent, the inn, the court, the camp, and the battle to paint the manners of his time. John tapped the side of his head, seeking the information he desired, canto vi—tap, tap went his fingers—stanza 17, wasn't it? *What a tangled web we weave, when first we practice to deceive.*

"This is not a noble war for Southern rights—this is murder," he voiced in a mournful tone. "And we deceive ourselves to think otherwise." It was a denial of Mosaic law, *Thou shalt not commit murder*. Nettie Slater, dear, beautiful Nettie; he'd fallen half in love with her already—she seemed to relish it most of all. This was not the kind of war John had been fighting along the Secret Line. This was not the kind of war he wanted to see. *Is this the only way to become a hero?* He clasped his palms together and searched the universe for an answer. *Commit cold-blooded murder?*

He brooded most of the night and slept fitfully, tossing and turning on the hard ground. He awoke the next morning, heavy-lidded and bone-weary. After a breakfast of bitter coffee, John, Nettie, and a few from the boat trip climbed aboard a platform car, pushed and pulled by four Negroes. On the hills, the white men would dismount and help push the car up the inclines. Then everybody, black and white, would jump on, as one Negro manned the break rod to slow the descent.

So it went, mile after mile. As they neared Ashland Station, a band of ragged men debouched from the woods with a rush. At first, the rail travelers could not fathom who these emaciated vagabonds were. Suddenly it dawned on them all.

"They're Union prisoners, escaped from one of our prisons!" Once again it was Nettie who gave voice to everyone's thought. Then she added one of her own: "Let's shoot the damned Yankees!"

Most of the men drew their revolvers and fired a fusillade right in the faces of the Union escapees. The rail car travelers shot their revolvers several times, careful to reserve a bullet for any of the Negroes who might hesitate in his work or rebel on behalf of the dying Yankees left along the track. John drew his revolver along with the others. But he aimed and fired over the oncoming Yankees' heads. Was this not akin to murder, too? Where would it all end?

CHAPTER 12

Arriving in Richmond, John and Nettie went to the Confederate State Department, where Secretary of State Judah Benjamin now commanded the Secret Service operations in the U.S. and Canada. John cooled his heels in an anteroom while Nettie met with Benjamin.

"This shouldn't take too long, Mr. Surratt," she cooed as she left. She still wore that blasted masque veil, but John envisioned her eyes sparkling. Her outcry of "Shoot the damned Yankees!" echoed in his mind. So much beauty propelled by so much malice. She attracted and repulsed him at the same time. *How could I feel so strongly for someone like this?* He questioned his own fantasy. Sure, she was stunning; no red-blooded male would argue with that.

But her nerve, her courage, her brash ways drew him to her. *Is this a reflection of who I am?* He delved into the depths of his soul for the answer, but it only led to more questions. Had seeing the most destructive side of war hardened him, rendering him immune to its horrors? Is that what drew him to her? Even a few months ago he'd have considered her a heartless monster. But now he saw the necessity of killing the enemy—because they were just as willing to kill him. It was kill or be killed—something Nettie Slater had learned long ago. But he still had a ways to go before he could call himself immune to the horrors. He still had a heart—a Christian heart at that—and he was a Christian before a Confederate.

If he stuck with her, she'd teach him about war—and about life. Boy, would that have made Pa proud! He would grow immune the longer this war dragged on, he had no doubt.

But what about after the war?

"Good afternoon, Mr. Surratt." Assistant Secretary of State Quinton Washington startled him. "Secretary Benjamin will see you now." He swept his hand in a graceful arc towards Benjamin's office. John knew the Secret Service operated under an act recently passed by the Confederate Congress, but Benjamin ran the whole operation by the seat of his pants. He was its only law, as befitted the only man to hold three successive cabinet offices in the Confederate government.

"Welcome back, Mr. Surratt!" Secretary Benjamin put down a half-eaten wedge of chocolate cake and dusted the crumbs off his hands. A smile came through his immaculately groomed beard in that ingratiating, yet irritating manner John remembered from his last visit. The Secretary managed to display seeming friendliness and sly insincerity at the same time. He and John shook hands. "Will you not join us in a drink?"

"Not for me, thanks." *Especially if it's sherry!* He glimpsed a crystal carafe filled with the syrupy liquid and fought a grimace.

"We're awaiting the arrival of some important guests. Ah! Here they come now."

Sergeant Harry Brogden entered and stood at attention. As he saluted, in walked His Excellency, Confederate President Jefferson Davis. John's breath halted. He stood at attention as if he were a soldier.

John knew Brogden from his trips along the Secret Mail Line, but he'd never met His Excellency President Davis. As Brogden made introductions, John stammered a, "H—h—hello, Your Excellency, sir," to President Davis's hearty greeting and handshake. He wondered if he should bow to his president. Oh, why not? He bowed. John calmed a bit as the president grasped his hand. He seemed like a regular guy after all.

President Davis's left eye was clouded over; John knew that His Excellency suffered from a condition brought on by shingles that plagued him. His eye miraculously cleared up whenever he traveled into the hinterland to join his troops.

Benjamin gave President Davis his own chair, motioned all to be seated, and stood to one side.

"Gentlemen," His Excellency began, "we are here today to modify our Campaign of 1865 in light of the desperate military situation facing the Confederacy. Secretary Benjamin and Assistant Secretary Washington are already familiar with the changes."

John noticed that President Davis blinked a lot.

"As you know, the Virginia Campaign was to be an effort to set General Grant back on his heels, allowing our General Lee to put his army on the cars and head for a unification of army commands with General Johnston in North Carolina. We would tear up the tracks behind General Lee's departing forces to prevent Union troops from following our men closely. The plan is to begin in April, the rainiest month in Virginia, to bog down General Sheridan's Federal cavalry on the dirt roads, turned or churned into mud by the attempted passage of thousands of horses and men." He stopped and cleared his throat. A lackey rushed up to him with a glass of something amber-colored. "Initially," he continued, "we had hoped to disrupt the Union command system through sabotage, disturbances against the Northern military draft, spreading infectious diseases through selected Union cities, destroying New York City by arson, and kidnapping Lincoln in exchange for our many men held captive in Northern prison camps. This part of the plan seems to have failed—no reflection on you or the men operating with you, Mr. Surratt, I assure you."

John tipped an imaginary hat.

"We now feel, in discussions with General Lee and Secretary of War Breckinridge, that there is no time to capture Lincoln or to obtain the release of our men held up North. So, I have turned to Secretary Benjamin and the Secret Service for assistance. Mr. Secretary, would you explain the new wrinkles in our plan to the sergeant and Mr. Surratt?"

"Certainly, Your Excellency," Benjamin fawned, nodding. "Perhaps y'all will remember the infamous Kilpatrick-Dahlgren Raid of last winter—almost exactly a year ago, in fact? We took a pile of papers off Dahlgren's body after a skirmish north of Richmond where he was killed. These documents outlined Lincoln's objectives, including capturing or *killing* President Davis and his whole cabinet. What we propose to do is to pay back Lincoln tit for tat." His speech slowed as he continued, "We have assembled a group of explosive experts under the command of Sergeant Frank Harney. Lewis Powell will smuggle these men and fifty pounds of black powder into Washington. There they will break into the White House basement, plant the explosives under the cabinet meeting room, set a horological fuse, and blow up the entire Union government, Abe Lincoln and all, in one clean blast."

"Lord Jesus!" John swore in a most unpriestly manner. He couldn't believe what he'd just heard. Maybe he wasn't so jaded after all.

"Brilliant!" Brogden applauded. John gaped at him, stunned.

"You, Mr. Surratt, and J. Wilkes Booth have been in the bowels of the White House on many occasions, I understand," Benjamin asserted.

John had trouble finding his voice. "Not I personally, but Booth and others have." He coughed and tried to even out his breathing. Lord above, what barbarians! Whatever happened to the genteel South? He answered his own question: invaded by the North in the War of Northern Aggression. *Kill or be killed.* He kept that in mind.

"Nonetheless, you will inform Booth that he and his party will be delegated to the task of getting Sergeant Harney to the right spot to do the Yankee administration the most harm," Benjamin continued. "Sergeant Brogden, you will be in charge of seeing to it that all our men get back into our lines safely via the Secret Mail Line. We have furloughed troops in position to assist you should the Federals pursue them."

"Well, that's all," Quinton Washington said. "We

will give you further orders later." Brogden saluted and withdrew from the room.

"And you, Mr. Surratt..." Washington turned toward him. "You will also escort Mrs. Slater who will take dispatches to Montreal to bring our operatives there up to snuff. Drop by first thing in the morning and the papers will be ready for y'all. Make haste with care!"

"Yes, sir." John knew he must obey these orders. But this was beyond atrocious. Blow up the White House? He still couldn't get over that. That was an extreme act. He racked his brain for an easier, more humane way.

He hadn't realized the South was that desperate. But no sense trying to talk them out of it. He'd appear a coward at best, a turncoat at worst. Much as it pained him, he had to keep his mouth shut.

Outside, the whine and thud of shells over besieged Richmond and Petersburg punctuated the dire necessity of John's mission.

Yes, he admitted as a dark foreboding enshrouded him. They *were* that desperate.

"How do we get back to the city from the river?" Nettie asked as John and Sergeant Brogden returned to the Potomac with her the next day.

"Maybe we can cross over at Brogden's camp to Chaptico and catch the Leonardtown stage," John suggested.

"Good idea," Brogden agreed. "It'll throw the Yankees off if you come in a different way. I'll have

Private Joe Baden row you across at dawn and you can meet the stage mid-morning."

~

And so it was done. Later, as they bounced over the rough rural roads of Southern Maryland on the stage to Washington, Nettie watched John, or rather John's book cover, as he hid his face behind it. She looked forward to a nice dinner and coaxing him out of his shell. He was a gentleman, all right, but his standoff-ishness stumped her. She tried not to take it as an insult. Why *hadn't* he tried to paw her? Land sakes, could he be one of those Nancy-boys?

Although she'd kept her distance and they hadn't shared much about their private lives and backgrounds, she knew they made a great team: same goals, same love for the South, same burning desire to see their side win. That's what brought them together in the first place. Oh, the priceless look on his face when he laid eyes on her for the first time! Of course he must've expected a bent-over old crone with wrinkles and a wart at the end of her nose, draped in widow's weeds. But when he feasted on her coal-black hair and shapely figure, he barely sputtered the password.

She would have been happy to strike up a friendly chat and exchange war stories, and even a few bawdy jokes, but she'd learned the hard way never to trust anyone right off. He'd come with impeccable references, but this was wartime—for all she knew, he was a spy under Lincoln's thumb. Some of her naïve colleagues now languished in POW camps because they'd trusted "honest-looking" men.

But she trusted him. He was on their side, all right, a loyal Confederate, she'd bet her life on it. And was she going to enjoy molding him to her touchstones. Like dipping a new brush in swirls of paint and stroking this way and that to create a work of art on a blank, untouched canvas. If anybody was untouched, it was this boy—even if they were the same age.

As if he could sense her gaze, he tossed a nonexistent lock of hair out of his eyes. He lifted his arm way up and scratched the back of his head, another nervous gesture. He always had to be doing something in her presence—scratching an arm, checking his watch, tugging on a sock, rubbing his hands together in a washing motion—he was so ill at ease with her, she felt sorry for him. She would make it her duty, with as much effort as she put into The Cause, to get John Harrison Surratt comfortable with her, until he no longer stuttered, stammered, blushed, or lost his voice whenever she came within pea-shooting distance.

"Dickens, hm?" She nodded, appreciating that side of him. He didn't seem the type to go in for literature; she reckoned his reading material ended at whatever catalog hung from a cord in the privy. "I like Dickens, too. Especially *Oliver Twist*. How did you get interested in his stories, Mr. Surratt?"

He lowered the prop. "My friend and fellow boarder at the house, Louis Weichmann. I've known him since we were young'uns, we went to seminary together. But now he works for the War Department. Has a whole shelf stuffed with those books written by hifalutin' authors, the Brontes, Shakespeare, and even some Greek stuff. He tried to explain *The Iliad* to me, but it just didn't catch my fancy. Shakespeare's more to my liking." He fanned the pages with his thumb. "I've been to see near half a dozen of John Wilkes and Edwin Booth's plays. I've never seen the oldest brother, Junius, though."

"Ah, yes, the Booths. John Wilkes is sultry and theatrical, but he makes it obvious he's acting. Edwin is much more seasoned. The craft seems to come more naturally to him. I've never seen Junius. Which Booth brother do you prefer?" She'd met Edwin in passing, but had never met the reportedly captivating and dashing matinee idol, John Wilkes, who had women swooning at his feet. Not her, though—she preferred the shy types—like John Surratt.

"Wilkes is the best actor I have ever seen," John gushed as he looked directly at her. "Even better than his brothers Edwin or Junius, I'll venture. Edwin's the poet, but Wilkes is the passionate one. He rips into his roles like he's really the person living it. Why, I once saw him as King Richard in a duel scene where he plumb drove Richmond off the stage and crashing into the orchestra pit!"

Practice for a future real-life duel, perhaps? she wondered. "Doesn't he get hurt playing scenes as intensely as that?"

"Yeah, my friend Davy Herold is a pal of Booth's. Says he's got scars crisscrossing his chest, arms, one on his cheek. Shows how serious an actor he is. Me, I could never act." He shook his head, his tone wistful. "I could be nobody but Little Johnny, I wouldn't know how to try to be anybody else."

Oh, yes, he was authentic, all right. No double agent would ever admit to all this. She gave him a reassuring wink. "You don't have to. You're best when you're just yourself." *Little Johnny*, huh?—all six foot three inches of him!

This brought a flush crawling across his cheeks. He let out an uneasy chuckle and hiked his book up over his face again, but his trembling hands made it clear he was not reading. So she'd broken some ice—a few icicles at least—this was the most they'd talked since they'd met.

"Mr. Surratt, where are we going when we exit at the District stage stop?" Now that she'd gotten him talking, she wanted to keep the conversation going, work her way up to his hopes and fears, pry his most secret desires out of him. He was a dam waiting to burst. She yearned to penetrate this mine of intrigue and possibilities.

He lowered the book and looked out the window. She followed his gaze, at the scenery whizzing by, the occasional farmhouse punctuating the flat fields, smoke streaming from chimneys, clothes fluttering on lines. "It'll be mealtime, I reckon. We can go to the restaurant across the street. They serve fancy vittles like duck, and everybody gets two forks."

She raised her fingers to her lips to hide her grin. "Sounds charming—and expensive."

"I got some government money for expenses." He patted his trouser pocket. "We don't need to take nothing from our pockets."

"Well, that's very generous of them to treat you to fine cuisine." But she doubted the government gave them a penny extra to indulge in such luxury. She knew the stingy politicians gave their couriers barely enough to stay alive. He just wanted to impress her. How gentlemanlike. None of the boors she knew would spring for more than a shot of cheap whiskey.

She tingled at the prospect of teaching him the inns and outs of intimacy. When she was finished with him, he'd be a man—with plenty to brag about. She quivered as goosebumps of anticipation prickled her arms.

She flashed him an inviting smile and batted her lashes. Soon he'd be chatting to her like an old friend, exchanging repartee, laughing easily, confiding in her, without the need to scratch his head or his arm or his foot or tug on his trouser legs.

A blast of wind slapped Nettie's face as she stepped off the rickety stagecoach and onto the platform. John buttoned his coat up to his chin and pulled his slouch hat down over his brow. The foul odors blowing off the drainage canal turned her stomach. But she looked forward to that fancy restaurant and eating with two forks.

The Metropolitan looked a mite seedy. She preferred the posh National Hotel, where important people stayed, like Booth. But it was quieter here than out on the Avenue. No shouting vendors or drunks singing in the streets like in the bustling Washington City. As they registered, she noticed two rooms on separate floors reserved for "Henry Sherman," the alias John frequently used in Richmond.

"We ought to have dinner early and lay low after." He removed his hat and smoothed his hair down till it looked glued to his head. She didn't know if this was another nervous gesture or an attempt to groom himself with no time to freshen up. She looked forward to a hot fragrant bath herself, but matters of war came first.

He made it obvious he intended to 'lay low' by himself when he stammered, "well...uh...good eve," and absconded to his room alone.

"Oh, well...there's always tomorrow night," she murmured. For now, she had the script of the racy play *Jane Shore* to keep her titillated.

~

The next morning, John met his mother in the lobby of the Metropolitan. They exchanged the perfunctory cheek kiss and she got right down to business.

"Do you know that there are Federal police spies at Pennsylvania House and the National Hotel, besides the ones in front of our own house? I hired a new wench at home, Susan Mahoney, she calls herself. Mighty high and fancy for a Negress, if you ask me. But I do not trust her. She spies for that swine Baker, Stanton's minion, I think. But I need the help, and she does show up."

"How do you know all that, Ma?" Suspicion crept into John's voice.

"I keep my eyes and ears open, unlike you and Booth and the others. I watch all the folk who walk the neighborhood. Wanderers and such have been nosing around my house servants. Even if Susan is not in Baker's employ, she would sell us for less than Judas sold Our Lord—you mark my words!" She gave a resolute nod. Her bonnet ribbons fluttered.

"Be that as it may, Ma, I have some important news that you must relay to Booth, when he returns from New York." In a lowered voice, John proceeded to tell her of Sergeant Harney and the plan to blow up the White House.

She didn't react with half the shock he had when he'd first heard it. Being married to Pa all those years, nothing surprised her anymore, he reckoned.

"It's sure the fastest way," was all she said, but a slow grin spread her lips. "I will tell him, but knowing Booth, he'll resent being relegated to a minor role in any scheme he's involved in."

"Yeah, but he won't throw a conniption fit in front of you, like he would for any of us others," John countered.

"Take care when you show up at the house. Remember what I told you about Susan Mahoney!" She turned and left John to his own devices.

As he took a solitary walk around the block, he pondered his mixed feelings. As a Southerner, he knew blowing up the White House and its most despicable inhabitant would be the best revenge for all the tragedy he'd wreaked upon the South. But deep down in his heart, as a Christian, he abhorred the heinous act. Was it any better than what the North was doing to them?

Oh, if only he didn't feel so torn so often! He sought the truth: *What is really driving me?* Desire to win, desire to please Pa...But so far removed from his first attempted vocation, the Church, he wondered if his "noble" acts would doom him and his cohorts to a hell crawling with Yankees.

He was in too deep to quit and be branded a coward. He pictured all those dead young soldiers, their blood soaking the battlefields. He didn't enlist, as he'd promised Ma—that made him coward enough. But he didn't dare back out of *this*.

CHAPTER 13

JOHN KEPT low while awaiting news from Booth but it wasn't easy. Restless and bored, he shuffled around the house, raiding the pantry to grab vittles, getting in his mother's and sister's way as they did their chores. "Make yourself useful, Johnny. Haul out the trash." He happily obliged. It gave him something to do.

The highlight of his days was hi-tailing it to the Post Office, hoping to retrieve a letter from the leader of their pack. On the third day, he bumped into Lou in the lobby.

"John!" Lou grabbed John's hand and pumped it with a vicelike grip. "I had no idea you were back in town!" He stepped back to get a gander at his dear friend. Fine gloves and leggings covered his hands and legs.

"Lou, ol' top, how are you?" John pulled his hand free and flexed his fingers.

"Doing quite well. Have you been up to the house? How long will you be staying?" He tripped over his words, his tone exuberant, as if they'd been separated for years.

"Not long. I'm lodging at the Metropolitan to

avoid Federal spies—excuse me just a minute." John stepped over to the cage.

"James Sturdy," John told the clerk. He went back to Lou, holding a letter written in atrocious penmanship.

"Who is James Sturdy?" Lou asked.

"You're looking at him." John handed the envelope to Lou and pointed to the New York City postmark.

"Is that the same one who stayed at your mother's —who later called himself the Reverend Paine?" He studied the envelope and looked up at John.

"None other." John took the letter back and slid it inside his jacket. "He went to Baltimore after leaving here, to see his girl and warn her father that our plot to kidnap the president failed." He lowered his voice. "The local Provost Marshal's office is constantly on their tails. So he went to New York City shortly after. Keeps the Feds off their guard, don't ya know? He expects Booth any moment now. A new scheme is cooking against the Federal high command. We still hope to use the information you gave us on the numbers and locations of Confederate soldiers in Federal prison camps. We'll win this war yet!" He pumped his fist in the air. "I'd holler a rebel yell, but this ain't the place." His eyes darted around the nearly empty Post Office.

"You mean the stuff that *you* took from my office during off-hours?" Lou frowned, his tone indignant.

John clapped Lou on the shoulder. "Old friend, you are in this as deep as anyone. If you do not believe me, go ask Secretary of War Stanton. You'll still be protesting your innocence as they slip the noose over your head and tighten it around your neck, I allow."

Those words made Lou choke. "John, don't even joke about something like that!" He gasped as if a noose did encircle his neck.

He followed John outside. At the curb, John approached a sleek, well-fed horse and mounted. "Well, thanks for the laugh anyway, Lou. That's a precious rarity these days." He spurred his mount and kicked up dust, leaving Lou there, coughing and sputtering.

~

Next eve before supper, Lou entered their room and handed John a telegram. "Mrs. Holohan brought this to my office. I reckon she couldn't wait till I got back here."

John read it to himself.

To Wickmann, Esq., 541 H Street,

Tell John to get the number and street at once.

J. W. Booth

John whooshed in relief and wiped his brow. "Well, it's about bloomin' time."

"What does it mean?" Lou sat at the edge of the bed.

"Sometimes you're too inquisitive for your own good." Now it was John's turn to sound indignant.

"We have to be that careful in our contacts, huh?" Lou countered.

John knitted his brows and uttered an annoyed, "Sheesh." Sometimes Lou just didn't know when to quit. "You better take a walk with me after supper so we can talk."

Later the two went down to Tenth Street and turned towards Ford's Theater. But they stopped a block and a half away at St. Patrick's School. John inquired for Miss Annie Ward, a family friend and teacher there.

"What did Mrs. Murray say?" John asked her, referring to the owner of the nearby Herndon House.

"She said that she would have a room whenever y'all needed it," Miss Ward said. "Go on down, she's expecting you."

"Thanks, Annie. You're a real doll." John forced nonchalance into his voice. Underneath he trembled. It was not his nature to compliment a lady this way.

Miss Ward blushed and excused herself.

"C'mon, Lou." The men walked down F Street.

"Where we goin'?" Lou asked as they crossed the road to the intersection with Ninth Street.

"Herndon House. It's a boarding house, but it's a business, not a come-as-you-may operation like Ma's." They climbed the porch steps and John knocked on the door.

A mulatto servant answered. "Mrs. Murray, please." John always made it a point to treat everyone with courtesy—even people of color.

When Mrs. Murray came out, John asked to speak with her privately.

"Huh? What for?" She glanced at Lou, then focused back on John.

"Perhaps Miz Annie Ward has spoken to you about...about engaging a room?" John kept his voice low. "A room for a delicate gentleman, who was to have his meals sent up to him? We need it for Monday the 27th this instant."

"Oh! Miz Ward!" She nodded. "Yea, she was here. Your room'll be ready at the appointed time. Send the gentleman over, no problem." She threw another questioning glance in Lou's direction and went back inside.

It didn't take long for Lou to suspect that the "delicate gentleman" was none other than that indelicate bruiser, Reverend Paine, or Lewis Powell, or whatever he called himself now.

"This concerns that Powell derelict, don't it?" Lou's voice quivered as he broke out in a cold sweat under his heavy layers of clothing.

"Aw, shucks, Lou. Don't look all wild-eyed and scared. We won't tell on you," John assured him. "The only person you have to be afraid of is you, yourself. Look, let's meet tomorrow evening at Kloman's for one of their oyster dinners they're so famous for. I will let you in on everything. It'll be just like old times, me and you, no one else. What do you say?"

A jumble of feelings pulled Lou in every direction —fear, affection, the desperate need to be useful. "I say let's!" A rush of anticipation lifted his spirits. "Finally, we'll be spending some time together." As they parted on the street, Lou wondered if he had unintentionally misled Major Gleason earlier, when he said the plot was over. *Should I go back and straighten out the record?* He pondered the decision. *No,* he decided seconds later. Gleason had heard him cry "wolf" one too many times. His credibility hung by a thread already.

Besides, he might as well hear what John had to say. He remembered John's ominous threat: "You'll still be protesting your innocence as they slip the noose around your neck." Lou's collar seemed mighty tight all at once. He loosened his tie and took a deep breath, expanding his chest, imagining the horror of strangling at the end of a rope. He suppressed a shudder. Dear God, what a way to go.

~

The next night, Lou sat in Kloman's Oyster House opposite John. "Ah, it's just like the old days!" Lou poured them each a glass of champagne that he'd paid for. After a hearty feast, also Lou's treat, they relaxed over brandy and segars. Neither really smoked, but it presented a sophisticated air, so they put on a good act for the public and themselves.

"To think that we might be whipped by that uncouth Illinois log-splitter," John pontificated. "Him and his arbitrary arrests, unconstitutional acts, confiscation of property, illegal appropriations without the sanction of Congress, policing the polls with soldiers to intimidate the voters..." He ran out of breath.

"Well, what is the news from Richmond about the military campaign?" Lou sipped brandy from the second round he ordered. "I trust Lee is doing better against Grant than you were with *Mrs*. Slater?" He wiggled his brows.

John ignored the dig. "It's all there, Lou. All in place. The notion is that Lee can move faster on the railroads to unite with Joe Johnston in North Carolina than Sheridan can push his cavalry through the mud to cut him off. Lee will tear up the tracks behind him. While Grant flounders in the mud, Lee and Johnston will join to defeat Sherman coming up from

South Carolina." He puffed on his segar and sputtered. "Then Lee will turn to hit Grant's army, strung out in pursuit." He coughed and gulped his brandy. "He will occupy the central position, able to turn and feint at will, while the Bluebellies will be unable to respond fast enough to save the day. That's a Napoleonic position, the middle between the enemies two forces, or so President Davis said."

"Where do *we* come in?" Lou tapped his segar against the table edge and flicked the ashes off.

John leveled a stare at him. "Now don't faint or yell or puke. This is for strong stomachs. This Sergeant Harney is planning to blow up the White House during a cabinet meeting. That will destroy Lincoln and the government's ability to control and coordinate the Yankee response. The Radical Republicans will be so caught up in their desire to take over the government by electing a new Secretary of State, they'll just spin their wheels like a locomotive on ice. And no one'll be willing to back down, to throw sand on the tracks, so to speak, to get everything moving again, until it's too late."

To John's relief, Lou didn't faint or puke. He didn't say a word at first, just sat glassy-eyed. He seemed to like what he'd heard. It gave John a renewed confidence in him. If only Lou could ride and shoot, he'd have let him join the blasted plot.

"It seems the timing of the campaign is already fouled up." Lou sounded calm and calculating. "Richmond has fallen and Petersburg, too. I think it's an effective act, and it needs to be done, but we're nowhere ready to act. What's'iz name...Harney...hasn't shown up yet."

"Yeah, it don't look good," John admitted. "Davis

and Benjamin swore they would hold on as long as they could. Harney is s'posed to come in across from the Virginia shore. He left a couple days ahead of us. The weather's been too dry. That bodes ill for Lee, if Sheridan's cavalry can move fast enough to cut the rails at Amelia Court House."

"So, did you have an enjoyable trip with the French woman?" Lou artfully changed the subject.

"Yeah, if you consider smelling her heavenly perfume a nice trip. We talked a little down to Port Tobacco. But it never gets further than that." He leaned closer. "I'll tell you a secret. Word is she's frigid. You know what that means?"

"Course I do." Lou snickered. "Figgers. The one bird you manage to get paired up with, and she's an ice princess. Well, maybe you can thaw her out. See if they can spare some of that black powder they're using for the White House."

"Ah, yeah, I'm halfway there already." John smirked, blinking rapidly, as he always did when he spun a tall tale. And this was taller'n the Washington Monument. "Thank heaven the bordellos are still the only institutions functioning smoothly in Richmond, huh?" John watched as Lou digested the remark and knocked back his brandy.

"Why are you going to Canada?" As John expected, Lou changed the subject back to business.

"I got to deliver dispatches and bring them up to snuff. Miz Nettie and I leave tomorrow." John forced the excitement out of his voice at the thought of being with her again. "I think I'll suggest that she stay in New York City. I can go through to Montreal myself, alone on the cars. I got ten $20 gold pieces from Benjamin. I exchanged $40 with Mr. Holohan, Ma's boarder, for greenbacks when I got a clean change of clothes. They spend with less fanfare. We came up on the Leonardtown stage. No rigs to rent and trace that-away. Made good time, got here in only two days. Took us just over three to get down to Richmond."

"So you're on a Christian name basis with, er...*Miz Nettie*, are you? A few more trips like that is enough time to thaw her out," Lou mused.

"Oh, yeah, right from the get go..." John caught himself blinking this time. "But she's all business—most of the time..." He trailed off, not wanting to embellish his acquaintanceship with Mrs. Slater too much—that would cheapen it. But she never seemed to warm to him anyhow—or did she? They had a nice chat on the stage ride up from the river. At least they had something else in common besides the war—Dickens novels.

~

Nettie sat in a shabby but comfortable wing chair in a corner of the Metropolitan Hotel's lobby, idly fingering a well-worn book off the meager one-shelf library. It was coincidently a copy of the same Dickens novel that John had been reading on the stage from Chaptico. But she was not reading the book. It was more for style—bait to attract the big fish she was about to reel in.

As she waited, Nettie mused over her spying and courier activities. This exciting phase of her life began early that year, when she delivered a letter to Confederate Secretary of War James Seddon:

House of Representatives
January 16, 1865

Sir;

We have the honor to ask for a passport for Mrs. Antoinette (Nettie) Slater of Salisbury, North Carolina, to pass the military lines of the Confederate States. She's a resident of Salisbury, but her mother, a French lady, resides in the city of New York. Mrs. Slater desires to return to her mother, where she can be more comfortably situated.

She has lost her only brother in the Confederate Army, and we have no hesitation in vouching for her loyalty and her high social position. We hope she will meet with no difficulty in passing the lines of our army.

We have the honor to be,

B. S. Gaither, Member of Congress

J. G. Ramsay, Member of Congress

On the back of the letter, which had been folded in thirds, was Major Carrington's reason for sending her to the Secretary:

Resp'y referred to the Hon. Sec. Of War.

My only reason for hesitating in giving this pass is that the husband of the applicant is in the Confederate service. The representations of the Hon. Mssrs. Gaither & Ramsay make a case for exception to the general rule.

I. H. Carrington

Jan'y 16/65 Provost Marshal

Seddon then let the letter flutter to the floor and gazed with open longing at its beautiful young courier standing before him.

He hardly knew the facts. For example, she had three brothers, two of whom had deserted the Confederate service. One of them had been charged with enticing others in his unit to leave with him.

But that was just the beginning.

She was born Sarah Antoinette Gilbert—pronounced in the French manner, with a soft sibilant 'g'—in Middletown, Connecticut, in 1843. Her parents came from the French West Indies, and the family spoke French as well as English; in Nettie's case, without a foreign accent in either. Her father manufactured pills, and bore the honorary title *Doctor*. He also taught French in a local high school. Her mother ran a rooming house, and Nettie provided little "extras" for the boarders, after hours. The family removed to Hartford and Nettie gave birth to a son out of wedlock.

Nettie's mother took the boy and her elder daughter to New York City. Disgusted with the whole affair, her father and brothers departed for Kinston, North Carolina. Initially, Nettie followed her mother. But eventually she, too, went to North Carolina, where she married a dance instructor, Rowan Slater. He suffered unfair ridicule because of his profession.

The War of Northern Aggression forced the newlywed Slaters to move to Goldsboro. Because the war generation shunned dancing, Rowan became a Confederate purchasing agent. Bored with that, he joined the army, and Nettie never saw him again.

No one but Nettie, of course, knew her life story.

But Secretary Seddon would not have cared if he had known her inside out. He merely suspected that the sweet creature standing before him was not as pure as she seemed.

The slim, delicate-looking young lady was built to please. Seddon ogled her a shade too long. She blushed and lowered her eyes demurely. Her fingers toyed with the ribbons of her fashionable straw hat with its heavy veil attached, no doubt to guard her privacy from the prying eyes of Richmond's lecherous soldiers, civilian contractors, and love-starved men like him.

"How would you like to make a little easy money?" Seddon proposed. "On your feet, not on your back."

"S-s-sir!" she stammered. "I did not come her to be insulted by low, vile creatures as yourself, posing as government bureaucrats. I *thought* you were a gentleman."

He retrieved the letter from the floor and folded it back up. "Save the theatrics, Mrs. Slater. I am not here to censure you. I have a proposition for you of some value to the Confederate government, your past notwithstanding. It would take someone with what I suspect is your background to pull this off." He paused with an inviting smile. "I want to employ you as a courier for the Confederate War Department, and possibly the State Department."

She raised a plucked brow. "Why me?"

"Hear me out, little lady," he insisted, still unable to tear his gaze away from her astonishing beauty. "The job is to carry dispatches from Richmond to Montreal by way of New York City. Each time you accomplish your assigned task, you will be paid in gold. A day or two with your New York family *en route* would seem in order. Are you interested?"

Nettie pondered it—for all of two seconds. "I'd be honored to serve the Confederacy in this way, Mr. Secretary," she readily accepted, all business, without a hint of flirtation.

CHAPTER 14

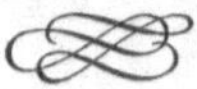

Now Nettie looked back on her short career
with fondness and an emptiness akin to loss, knowing
it would not last much longer. The South foundered
on her last pegs. *She* could see that, even if men like
Seddon couldn't face the truth. This was her third
trip, traveling with John Surratt, for Major General
Breckinridge. John fell all over himself trying to act
the gentleman, holding out his arm for her, doffing his
hat nearly every time she spoke, fawning like a
preening peacock. His theatrics charmed her.

Too bad John had no guts to act on his fantasies.
So she'd have to be the one to act on them.

She looked up as John came in from his dinner.
"Mr. Surratt!" She gave him a finger-wave.

"Why, Miz Nettie!" He approached, clearly
struggling to appear calm.

She stood and linked her arm through his. "Aren't
you going to escort me to my room? Come now, you
didn't help me down from the stage or hold my seat
for me in the restaurant," she flirted shamelessly. "I
have had to eat several meals in my room, all alone
and lonesome. Didn't your mother teach you how to

be a gentleman?" Her jaunty tone carried a hint of chiding.

He scuffed his foot back and forth, reminding her of a little child who's been reprimanded. He did have a lot of little-boy qualities. Some were cute and endearing. Some were just—childish.

But he sure made her laugh. All in all he was delightful. "Oh, *John*." Using his given name for the first time, she touched his cheek with her ungloved fingers. He didn't flinch. "I'll be happy to teach you the fine points of etiquette. We'll start now. Walk me to my room and wait until I'm safely locked inside."

But she had no intention of locking him out. She'd already abandoned her earlier idea of going to their separate rooms to freshen up, call for a bath, change into lounging clothes. Still enjoying a nice warm buzz from the dinner wine, she abandoned her few inhibitions in the lobby. Forget perfume and the flimsy negligee or waiting until midnight to surprise him at his door. She couldn't wait another minute.

Arms still linked, she led the way up the stairs and down the third floor's corridor. The carpet was so threadbare, their footsteps made clicking sounds. This was hardly the fanciest place she had ever stayed in. But with better accommodations, she could cozy up to this courier business.

At the door of Room 314, she turned to face him. He fidgeted, his eyes on her key, plainly waiting for her to plunge it into the lock and vanish, so he could cut and call it a night.

But she had other plans for this boy-man. She slowly slid the key into the lock and turned it. The door swung open to a tastefully decorated room, a four-poster bed its focal point. Velvet draperies closed out the evening chill. A stove stacked with wood waited to blaze into life. *Oh, yes, that would be a nice touch.* Forget the bed, she could teach him all he needed to know in front of a roaring fire.

"Come in for a nightcap." She beckoned him inside. At first she felt the tug of resistance, but he meekly followed her in, taking small steps, glancing around as if hoping some of his cohorts would magically pop out of the walls with a bottle of whiskey and a deck of cards.

"It's all right." She closed and locked the door behind them. "Tell me, honestly, John. Have you ever been alone with a woman before?"

His head bobbed up and down. "Sure, lotsa times."

What a load of hokum. No man of the world would have put it that way. She couldn't imagine John Wilkes Booth, for example, describing his conquests as "lotsa times."

"Then you'll know just what to do, won't you?" She slid her shawl off her shoulders and it spilled onto the floor.

He started to bend to pick it up. She stopped him. "Leave it."

She removed his jacket and tie. "Hot, isn't it, John?" she whispered in his ear.

"A little. I am sweatin' if you want to know the truth."

"But I really would like you to light a fire," she cooed. "It'll add to the ambiance."

"You don't need ambiance, Miz Nettie. I don't know what it means, but it sounds French, and anything that sounds like that, you sure got loads of." He tittered, covering his mouth with his hand.

She smiled, slipping out of her shoes. "Let's dispense with the formalities. I'm just Nettie to you. So would you mind setting that kindling aflame?"

He dropped to his knees with a Lucifer, and soon the wood in the little iron stove blazed brightly, throwing out waves of heat.

Without letting him get to his feet, she knelt behind him and began kissing his neck. "Give me a minute and I'll get these skirts and crinolines offa me, but it'd be a mite nicer if you give me a hand—or two," she purred.

John turned to face her. "M—Miz Nettie," he stammered, wiping sweat from his brow. "I don't quite feel right here in your room while you disrobe, ma'am." He inched backward, knocking over the propped-up andiron. It crashed to the floor.

"Now how do you propose to get romantic with all our garments on?" Her skirt and crinoline fell away and pooled on the floor around her. She stood in only her petticoats.

He scrambled to his feet and groped behind him as he backed up towards the door. "Miz Nettie, this ain't right, what's between us is...to me, it's sacred and..." He gasped for air. "I respect you too much to take advantage of you in any way... I, in fact, planned to save myself for marriage, if'n you can wait till the war ends, and we can talk about it then, but I had designs on the priesthood so if that don't happen..." he rambled on and on in the same breath. She rolled her eyes and bent down to retrieve her garments.

"Well, nothing's happening tonight, as you made it crystal clear." The moment completely ruined and the notion of romance destroyed, her ardor shriveled as if he'd dumped a bucket of cold water over her head. "But thanks for coming clean and being honest, John. I don't hold it against you that you claimed you'd been alone with women 'lotsa times' and now admit you're an innocent. I respect you, too. But for marriage..." She climbed back into her crinoline and skirts. "I'm already married, though my husband may be dead, but I don't reckon another marriage is in the cards for me. I'm flattered by your proposal anyways, roundabout as it was." Fully dressed once again, she headed for the door to see him out, but he pulled it open and beat a hastier retreat than the Yankees at the First Battle of Bull Run.

The next morning, John and Nettie rushed to the Washington Railroad Station. The porter, pulling their luggage in a handcart, struggled to keep up. Too late for breakfast at any of the local road houses, they'd need wait for chow. "It would be nice to have dining cars on trains," John grumbled as his stomach growled.

When they arrived in New York, Nettie handed him a thick envelope. "Give these to General Edwin Lee." He helped her load her two trunks into a taxi and panicked...*do I kiss her hand?* He couldn't waste a second. She climbed into the taxi.

"Wait, Nettie!" He bounded up to her and grabbed her hand in an awkward gesture of affection. "Uh...about last night, um... I hope you're not mad at me... I want to see you again...and not just as partners in the war effort. I mean...when will I see you again?"

Her eyes expressed more pity than anticipation of their next meeting. "In these unpredictable times, when we don't know if we'll see another day, it's futile to plan for a future that may never be. Till then, take it one day at a time. God bless the Confederate States of America." She slipped her hand from his grasp. "Let's go!" she commanded the driver, leaving John standing there, empty and lovesick.

He tried to force her from his mind, but couldn't. Dragging his feet, he turned and wandered the streets of the bustling metropolis, trying to shake off his feelings of forlorn abandonment. Never had he been so smitten. *Is this true love?* It had to be. No emotion had ever consumed him so.

Figuring John Wilkes Booth was in town, he went to Edwin Booth's East Nineteenth Street brownstone and knocked on the door. A young black servant answered.

"Good day. Is Mr. Wilkes Booth in?" John peered inside. The waxed floor gleamed. A crystal chandelier glittered in the foyer. The sweet honeyed scent of beeswax wafted outside.

"No, sir." The servant shook his head. "Mr. Wilkes was here yesterday but no longer."

"Thank you anyway." John turned and wandered the elegant neighborhood, never feeling so alone. Nothing could be solved in New York. He considered following Nettie, but knew she'd hide her trail well. The address she gave the cabman was undoubtedly a ploy to get rid of John and conceal her tracks from the Feds.

He took the evening train to Montreal and arrived there early the next morning. Feeling somewhat renewed at the change of scenery, he registered at the rebel-filled St. Lawrence Hotel under his usual pseudonym, "John Harrison." That afternoon he gave Nettie's dispatches to General Lee.

"These detail some independent drafts to place your finances separately from Mr. Thompson, sir," John said. "There are some new directions on the revised spring campaign of this year."

John planned to claim that General Lee gave him a week to rest up before sending him on a new mission to Elmira, New York, to gain information about the layout of its infamous stockade holding thousands of Rebel prisoners of war. But John never went to Elmira. Someone else did—a tall man with dyed red hair who appeared in several haberdasheries and hotels using the name "John Harrison." Instead, John Surratt sat in Montreal, safe from arrest back home, awaiting Booth's summons to return to Washington, help get Sergeant Harney into the White House basement, and plant the explosives.

While he waited, John wrote his mother a short note, telling her that he would be in Canada indefinitely on business. A week later, he wrote a longer letter, detailing his boredom and the high cost of room and board in Canada, $2.50 per day in gold. To pass the time and get his mind off Nettie, he attended Mass in the local cathedral and splurged on a French pea coat, paying $10 in silver. He posted the letter to Annie Ward, who brought it over to Mary.

That evening, April 9th, the news of Robert E. Lee's surrender hit Washington City. When General Grant's army overwhelmed the thin Confederate defense line, Lee had no choice but to retreat from Richmond and Petersburg to save what was left of his army.

Overjoyed war-weary citizens, black and white,

danced in the streets, cheering and whooping. Fireworks exploded over the city.

But in Southern streets and homes, people mourned their loss.

"Here." Mary Surratt thrust the newspaper into her daughter's hands. "You read it out loud. I'm too disturbed at John's absence to read it myself. And I'm sickened by the whole thing." She grasped her rosary beads in her tightened fist.

But Annah, devastated over their crushing defeat, couldn't bear to read it. She crumpled the paper up and flung it into the fire.

On April 10, Canada received the shattering news of Lee's surrender. The next day, John received an urgent request from Booth: "I need you. Return to this den of iniquity at once. Delay not an hour." Back in Washington, John stayed clear of his mother's boarding house and possible Federal agents. Instead he went to the Herndon House and called on Lewis Powell in his "secret" room.

"We're all meeting here this very evening at six," Powell informed him, handing him a segar.

"But why?" John puffed on the segar and coughed. "To hear about another blunder in the making? This one had better be good," he spoke through gritted teeth. "It's too late to *abduct* Lincoln now."

Not a minute later, Booth entered and removed his hat with a flourish. "Speak of the devil, and I don't use the term loosely," John muttered under his breath.

"John my boy! How good to see you." Booth sauntered up to John and extended his hand. They shook. "I've sent Davy Herold to bring George Atzerodt here to our rendezvous. I was over at the National Theater." He lit a segar and puffed on it, holding it between his thumb and pointer finger. "I asked Manager Hess if he was going to illuminate tonight, and he said 'certainly.' Then I hinted he ought to invite the president. 'Yes!' and he snapped his fingers. 'Thanks for reminding me, Mr. Booth, I must send that invitation.' Fine work, hah, boys?" Booth chortled.

Powell answered a knock at the door and Atzerodt entered, Herold at his heels.

Herold noticed John and did a double take. "What are you doing here?"

"I know, I know, I'm supposed to be in Canada." John sat up straight. "But I'm here. Plans kind of got bollocks'd up. I went—"

"Quiet now! Listen up," Booth cut in. "I have news...I heard there was a clash between Mosby's men and the Eighth Illinois cavalry a couple of days ago at Burke's Station, down in Virginia."

"They're one tough outfit." Powell leaned against the window frame and crossed his arms. "We always hated to mix with them boys."

"What does that mean to us, Booth?" John braced himself for an answer he wasn't going to like.

"Well, the Yankees think it was a standard Mosby horse and mule raid." Booth paced the room. The others cleared the way for him. "But I suspected that it involved our man, Harney, and his escort. So I went over to the Old Capitol prison this morning and bribed a guard with a bottle. He said that several of Mosby's men were there, recent arrivals. He didn't know Harney's name, but he did think that one of the Rangers was an ordinance man. He said that the prison commandant was very suspicious, but that no one had talked yet. Everyone claimed that it was just an ordinance delivery that got out of Richmond before it fell."

Booth sat in the only empty chair and crossed his legs. "I stopped at my girlfriend Ella's sister's whorehouse on the way back. Met an Illinois officer fresh in from the Eighth, relaxing with a drink. Nice, loose-mouthed fella. I chatted a bit with him about the war. Then I asked how he and his boys were faring. He said that his Illinois boys had scattered a Mosby party at Burke's. Picked up a loose pack animal with twenty-five pounds of black powder on his back. A slew of the stuff spilled all over the road, and another mule with busted packs. Now, if that don't smell like Harney, then what does?"

"Dat means dat ve die Vhite House vill not blow up?" Atzerodt's query indicated to John that everyone was up to snuff on the alterations to the Virginia campaign, before Lee's surrender.

"What it really means is that we will have to carry out Harney's mission for him," Booth explained.

Alarmed, John approached Booth, desperate to talk him out of this deranged plot. "George is right, though. We cannot blow up the White House! We lack the talent to set off such an explosion without killing ourselves in the process." Trembling, he halted before Booth, almost toe to toe.

Booth's piercing eyes focused on a spot across the room. He stood and John stepped out of his way.

Booth paced silently for a heartbeat, then another. John held his breath, awaiting Booth's answer, wanting to shake it out of him.

"Right," he finally said, in a matter-of-fact tone.

John let out a whoosh of relief. Glory be, he'd persuaded the vainglorious John Wilkes Booth to abandon his insane plan. Now *that* should make history books!

"That's why we are going to assassinate the whole Union government—*individually*—with the same effect of Harney blowing up a cabinet meeting." Booth stared down each man as if daring one of them to defy him.

That declaration nearly knocked John over. *Lord Jesus, he's even crazier than I thought.* John shook his head in disbelief. This time he didn't even try to argue. The man was a lunatic, plain and simple.

Herold and Atzerodt stood there dumbfounded. John knew that blowing something up was fun to them—it was not murder, except in a sort of a detached manner. A body did not have to look his victim in the face, risk opposition. Instead it was just *bang!* and the whole matter was finished cleanly, except for the disintegrating carcasses of the victims, but then no one really *saw* that. It just happened. But a knife or a pistol was downright personal.

"That's quite a plan, Booth." John didn't want to voice his true opinion. Knowing how impetuous Booth was, he just might pull that Colt on *him!*

"So, how will this be carried out, Cap?" Powell's eager tone sickened John.

John knew that it made no never mind to Powell if the victim was one, ten, or a hundred feet away. Fighting on a Civil War infantry firing line did that to a man. Powell had wiped the gore and brains of many a companion or enemy off his tunic between Williamsburg and Gettysburg. One more time would not make any appreciable difference to him. John shuddered.

"Always to the point, Powell." Booth's sinister

smirk made John's flesh crawl. "Now, here is the lay of the political land. The whole Confederacy is hanging on out there, somewhere in the Piedmont of North Carolina. The government is probably around Danville, just north of the Virginia line. Joe Johnston's army was near Goldsboro, the last I heard. Lee surrendered, true, but he had only 25,000 men with him. Where are the rest?"

"I lay they all ran away. Deserted." Herold hung his head, his voice defeated. John marveled at the youth's accidental wisdom.

Booth ignored him. "I put it to you that they're on their way to Johnston right now. That means the Union government and its communications and leadership, right here in Washington, are still a prime military target. I have it on good word that General Grant has come to the city to regale Lincoln and his cabinet. What a target!" Booth flashed his signature sinister grin. "Powell, you must get into Seward's house," he continued, his eyes blazing. "He's confined there because of a carriage accident last week, seriously injured. That's our biggest problem. He has a grand old house of three floors, maybe an occupied attic on top of that. Gain entry any way you can and finish him off."

"Sure, why not?" Powell shrugged, as if Booth'd offered him a shot of whiskey. John cringed. He'd grown somewhat fond of Powell, a personable enough fellow. But now he plainly declared he was just another madman.

"I will personally take out Lincoln and Grant at the theater." Booth clutched at his lapels. "George..." He addressed Atzerodt. "You will shoot Vice President Johnson—and I mean shoot to kill."

"Oh, no!" Atzerodt waved his hands through the air, visibly shaking. "I am not villing to kill, a person to murder."

Booth spat in sudden rage. "You pigeon-livered white trash!" Then he calmed just as quickly. "Will you assist us, then? All you need do is show us the road to Indiantown in the dark. If you are unwilling, it will go bad for you."

Booth and Powell both gave Atzerodt a hard look. He quailed under their gaze.

"I vill all I can on die road to do." His voice shook. He wiped spittle from his lips.

"Then get yourself a horse and ride out to Benning's Bridge and wait for us. We will go to Surrattsville and then through Tee Bee to Bumpy Oak. Herold doesn't think he can find the road after dark. Can *you*?" Booth aimed a finger at Atzerodt like a pistol.

"Ja, I do it." He nodded, now looking eager to please his leader. "Maryland Point and die Nanjemoy are on der most direkt weg nach Virginia."

"All right, then, Herold will take out Johnson. Right, Davy?" Booth's gaze landed on Herold.

John could see Herold was no more enthusiastic than Atzerodt to kill anyone, but after Booth's threatening tone with the German, he didn't dare show cowardice.

"Sure, Cap." He gulped, wide-eyed, shaking with fear.

"No, no, I was just teasing. John Surratt will do it." Now he turned to John. "And I can depend on you, my good man, can I not?" he challenged, sounding more like a dare.

"Of course you can." John forced a smile, clasping

his hands together so no one could see them trembling. Ever the actor, Booth made a show of his contempt for the weaklings, Atzerodt and Herold. Yet John wondered, *am I any stronger than they? Does Booth know how pigeon- livered I am?* Of course he'd never admit it. He had to go along with the plan. He didn't dare quit.

"Davy, I want you to go out to Huntt's place down to Tee Bee, and pick up our horses there," Booth barked his orders. "We will stop for you after we strike Lincoln and the others. We will stop and get our stuff from Lloyd—you need not bother."

"What if Lincoln don't cooperate?" Herold again showed the common sense that seemed to elude Booth, John observed. "You *know* he don't keep appointments, Cap. We missed him two or three times already."

"Don't be such a pessimist," Booth snarled. "He would not dare miss this engagement, being with General Grant and all."

"But..."

"All right! All right!" Booth's voice thundered. "If we do not show by midnight, we will not need those horses any longer. You can bring them into the city tomorrow. I already got a buyer for the bay, anyhow— Mr. Greenawalt," Booth answered Herold's look of inquiry. "He offered me a fabulous $140—and I think that Judge Parker will take the other two," he went on. "We must all be ready at eight o'clock tonight. If all goes right, Powell will check with me and I will estimate the right time to shoot. Sometime after eight o'clock. You, Davy, may as well leave for Tee Bee right now. We will meet you at Huntt's store, not Thompson's like last time. Huntt has the horses." Booth clapped his hands together once. "Well, now, let's get cracking. You, too, George."

Herold and Atzerodt left the room and clomped down the stairs.

"Gentlemen, I'm going out to change into riding clothes. I will come back and pick you all up. Powell, I'll show you where Seward's house is. Then I'll meet you, and we can ride out of town, together, after the deed is done," Booth issued his final instructions.

"Yes, Cap," they agreed in unison.

"I sure am glad you're back, John." Booth's tone carried a note of sincerity. "I really need an extra hand I can rely on. Vice President Johnson will be over at the Kirkwood House, but meet me here with Powell, so we can coordinate times together."

"Right." A cold shiver went up John's spine the deeper Booth's plans sank in. *Please, dear God,* he silently prayed, *let the actor fail miserably—make someone stop him.*

Then he entertained a likely possibility: Lincoln wouldn't even go to the theater! With all the president had on his mind, he didn't have time for such frivolities. Booth was just being his theatrical, melodramatic self.

With that comforting thought, John's breathing calmed. Booth approached him and shook his hand, then shook with Powell and beat a hasty exit.

John went over to John Howard's imposing brick livery stable to rent a horse. Powell would use the big brown, blind of one eye, that Booth came over on. As Powell stood on the walk out front, Booth rode up, armed to the teeth, a sword dangling at his side like a war general.

"Y'all can go back to your rooms. Plans have

changed. I just learned from some Yankee staff officers down at the National Hotel that Lincoln and Grant will not show tonight. I'll call on y'all tomorrow. Hand over your horse, Powell." He wiggled his fingers in a 'gimme' gesture.

Powell dismounted and handed Booth the reins. "She's all yours, Cap."

"Where-all you off to now?" John asked.

"I reckon I ought to call off Atzerodt. No need to leave him out alone. He might get real angry or real drunk and blab everything. I can ride out and get Herold in the morning." Booth mounted and rode off eastward toward Benning's Bridge.

If this ain't just dandy, I don't know what is. John expelled a long whistle. *Foiled, again! Whew! My prayers are answered! Thank you, God.*

Relief flooded his body, soul and psyche alike, with an underlying impatience to get this whole thing over with. He nodded to Powell, turned his horse away fast, and rode back to the stable, desperate for a privy.

CHAPTER 15

THE NEXT MORNING, after a fitful night's sleep, John stepped into Booker & Stewart's Tonsorial Parlor. Charlie Wood, the most in-demand barber in town, stood at his chair giving one of his well-reputed shaves and haircuts to John Wilkes Booth. Michael O'Laughlin and a bearded man hovered around him.

"Mornin', John," Booth called out. John approached the men and they exchanged greetings.

"Say, Charlie, did you notice a scar on Booth's cheek when you put the chair cloth on him?" O'Laughlin asked in a seriocomic tone.

"Yea, now that you mention it, I did." Wood peeked under the steaming towel around Booth's face.

"They say that it was a boil that had to be lanced," John chipped in. "But I have it on good word that it really was a pistol shot."

"Nah, he must have got a little too far up front that time," O'Laughlin mused.

"Why, look at it," John urged. "He near lost his head!"

As Wood finished up, Booth laughed heartily with the others, rose from the chair, gifted the barber with a generous tip, and strolled into the street. The others followed at his heels. John brought up the rear, refusing to be another Booth kiss-up.

"I brought Davy Herold back in from Tee Bee this morning." Booth stopped to light a segar. "You gents stay available for another try tonight," he intoned like a suggestion, but it was clearly an order.

John stopped at Willard's for a beer, and as he entered a voice called out, "Hey, John!"

"Davy," John answered, as David Herold came over with another man he'd never seen before.

"This is Scipiano Grillo. John Surratt," Herold introduced them.

"We come over to see if General Lee was here." Herold glanced around. "Heard that he was."

"Nope." John shook his head. "They wouldn't let prisoners run loose, 'specially one as important as Lee."

"You ain't seen Booth, have you?" Herold lowered his voice and edged over to John as he spoke.

"'Fraid not." John kept his voice low, too, casting Herold a cautious glare. He'd have to give the boy a warning about mentioning Booth in the presence of strangers.

"You *are* goin' tonight, ain't you?" Herold's voice rose a tad too high.

John nodded. "Of course. Now you must excuse me—I have some business to attend to before then." He hastened onto Fourteenth Street and turned south to Pennsylvania Avenue.

The crowd of strolling passersby slowed his pace. John turned as General Ulysses S. Grant and his wife jingled by in an open carriage, the back piled high with baggage. Several staff officers escorted them.

A familiar voice yelled from behind as John crossed Tenth Street. Galloping hooves pounded the ground.

"John! Wait up!" Booth called out from astride his bay mare, wild-eyed and pale as a ghost. He pulled his mount up and leaned over. "I just witnessed several hundred of our captured officers being marched to Old Capitol Prison." He pressed the back of his hand to his forehead. "Great God! I no longer have a country! This is the end of constitutional liberty in America."

"There's not a danged thing any of us can do, Booth," John lamented in sympathy with his captured brothers. He lowered his head. "Not a thing."

"We'll get our revenge on the damn Yankees later. For now, listen up." Booth nudged John with the toe of his boot. "Things are coming rapidly to a head."

John looked up. "Is that General Grant's carriage?" His eyes followed the elegant barouche as it rumbled down the street.

"Yes, that's Unconditional Surrender Grant, all right, and the timing couldn't be more impeccable. They're heading to the B & O Railroad station." He waved in that direction. "Can you get over there posthaste? I can't let him get away."

John blanched. "You want me to shoot him at the station?"

"No, no." He swatted the air with his hand. "Follow him on the train and wait 'till around ten or ten-thirty tonight. Do him in at an opportune spot. You know, where you can get away. Then keep going north. I'll meet you at St. Albans Saturday or Sunday night. I think the train out of New York City is called the Midnight Express."

"I know it. I will get on it, right off." His mouth dry, he tried not to stammer.

Booth turned his horse about and called over his shoulder, "I'm headed for Ford's Theater. I'm confident that Grant won't live out the night. If anyone can do the job, it's the intrepid John Surratt. The South will forever be in your debt, sir."

John beat a hasty retreat. A jumble of disturbing thoughts and emotions assaulted him. At least he was not expected to kill the Vice President in a hotel room. He could abandon Booth's idiotic substitute-for-Harney scheme with ease and actually pursue a real military target: the Commanding General of the Union Armies.

Now this would be a heroic act—if he could handle the guilt that haunted him and the fear that terrified him. But the suffering of his beloved war-torn South broke his heart. Any other Southerner would agree—avenging Dixie this way greatly outweighed the guilt. The trepidation was far harder to overcome.

He needed to catch the 6:00 train. As he strode down Tenth Street, he saw his childhood friend David Reed in front of Steer's Sewing Machine Store. John nodded and doffed his new hat. Not seeming to recognize him at first, David looked twice, then gave him an admiring look. John found this amusing as well as a boost to his esteem; David wasn't the only one who'd done a double-take when seeing him on the street. Now that he was making some real money, he'd splurged on good duds, like today's tailor-made ensemble—suede jacket, fawn colored trousers, wide-brimmed slouch hat, and brass spurs with blue rowels that clinked a merry tune as he continued his jaunty stride. He couldn't bring himself to brandish a shiny walking stick, though. He didn't want to look *too* much like Booth.

John crossed the broad avenue and headed towards the stables.

"Doc?" John called out to the manager, veterinarian William Cleaver, who'd rented horses to John and Booth many times. "Doc..." He entered the paddock area. "I need a horse to get to the railroad station fast! But you'll have to come with me so I don't miss my train. I have no time to turn him in."

Cleaver pointed to a dark sorrell. "Sure, John. Grab that one standing at the hitch rack next to mine and let's go."

At the station, John slid off Cleaver's sorrel and hit the ground running.

"Board!" the conductor shouted, "All aboard!" The engine snorted two blasts on its steam whistle and with a clanging bell the 4-4-0 American-style locomotive began to spin its wheels. Smoke chuffed from its balloon stack. The drivers caught the steel rails and the train moved forward with a jerk. John took a running leap onto the end of the last car, clambering up the steps onto the platform.

"Nice job, sonny." The conductor helped John into the car. "I'll collect your ticket money in a bit. This coach is under special security. General and Mrs. Grant is aboard. Along with some of his military staff. I need to escort you forward with an armed guard."

"You don't say." John tried to sound surprised. "The illustrious General Grant on this very train? Well, no problem, sir."

"Got any firearms?" The conductor eyed John up and down.

"Just a four-barreled Sharps pocket pistol." He patted his pocket.

"Hand it over." He held out his palm. "We'll return it when we get to Baltimore or you can move to another car. Then we'll return it when you pass out of the car. No armed men allowed in here but the soldiers."

John looked past the conductor down the car, every seat taken with passengers and soldiers. No way he could shoot Grant here and survive. "I will move to another car forward, if you do not mind." He handed the pistol over.

"Here is his personal sidearm." The conductor gave John's gun to a uniformed officer. "This here's Grant's Chief of Staff Colonel John Rawlins. He will pass on forward."

Rawlins took John's pistol and led him forward down the aisle. General and Mrs. Grant sat on the left, Grant so close, John brushed against him. Across from him and surrounding him sat several officers, local dignitaries, and railroad executives. One of the soldiers, a captain, followed John down the aisle, revolver in hand.

At the end of the car, John went out on the platform and jumped over to the next coach. Rawlins returned his pistol and re-entered the rear car. The captain followed, backing in and not holstering his revolver until he had closed the door behind him. A heavy curtain covered the window, concealing the passengers within.

I can get Grant on the next train, John assured himself, fighting a stab of terror that shook him. But the next train had a special car assigned to its rear. Several soldiers armed with bayoneted rifles stood on its front and rear platforms, in addition to Grant's personal party inside. Curtains covered all its windows. No one could see inside, even after dark.

Even if John dropped all the guards, he would have to reload his pistol, assaulting the door to Grant's car.

"It's hopeless," a spectral voice whispered in his ear. "Not meant to be."

Eyes closed, John heaved a deep breath and exhaled. With wobbly knees, he staggered over to a bench and collapsed, physically and emotionally drained. An unbearable burden fell from his shoulders. He did not have to commit suicide to shoot Grant after all. No, this was not meant to be. Because the events spun completely out of his control, he wouldn't be branded a coward. He'd done all he could for his beloved South—so he wouldn't return home under the wrenching torments of guilt and shame. He could meet Booth at the Canadian boarder with a clean conscience. Better yet, he could meet his Maker and Lord Jesus Christ the same way—no hero, but no sinner either.

~

Longing for a warm hearth and the comfort of a home-cooked meal, John went home to his mother. After this traumatic event, he no longer cared who saw him or about lying low. He spent one night of peace and quiet before his next journey, to St. Albans, Vermont.

Still exhausted from his close brush with infamy, he took a train to New York City and checked into a cheap hotel near the depot. He planned to crawl into a bed and sleep around the clock. Then he'd push on to Vermont.

But the next morning, loud anxious voices woke him. He glanced at his pocket watch—eight-forty. Wondering what the ruckus was about, he dressed and went down to the small lobby. Clusters of people gathered around open newspapers. Women wailed hysterically. Every face looked contorted with agony or stunned with disbelief.

Baffled, he approached the nearest group and tapped a man on the shoulder. "Sir, what happened?"

"You haven't heard the news?" The gentleman gave John a queer suspicious look.

"No, I've not." Lord's sakes, what could it be?

"Why, President Lincoln and Secretary Seward have been assassinated." His voice broke.

John staggered back, nearly losing his footing. Regaining his senses, he shook his head. "It's too early in the morning to get off such jokes as that!"

"It's so." The gent then held up a newspaper and jabbed a finger at the screaming headline. John stared at the large black letters till they blurred before his eyes. He blinked and ran his eyes over the column, trying to take it all in—shot at Ford's Theater, expired this morning...

No names were mentioned, so it couldn't be Booth or any of his cohorts. He'd never heard anything regarding assassination spoken of during his entire time with them.

He turned and leapt back up the stairs. He locked himself in his room and sank into the mattress, head in hands. After all the mishaps and blunders that bordered on comic farce, he believed Booth would give up out of frustration or impatience, or maybe even come to his senses and give up on capture, abduction, blowing up the White House. But as he recalled that newspaper article, the truth struck him like a blow to his head with a sledgehammer: *Ford's Theater*. Who else but that deranged actor would have committed such a heinous murder in full view of a packed house?

He sat for what seemed like hours, disjointed thoughts and questions running through his mind. How did Booth finally get to Lincoln? Why wasn't a bodyguard protecting him? Why couldn't doctors save him? Did he suffer? How were his wife and sons dealing with this tragedy? Part of him still didn't believe it actually happened and that Lincoln was dead. He sat in such shock, it couldn't sink in.

A vivid image of the lanky bearded man formed in his mind's eye. John never hated Lincoln—not enough to see him murdered. But as Booth lured him further into that atrocious plot, he followed—enthralled, embroiled in the excitement of making history and avenging the South. Booth had cast his evil spell over them all. Now, in the aftermath, he began thinking clearly—and with that clarity of thought came a hideous self-loathing. Could he ever forgive himself for his actions? After all, his mother had raised him to know right from wrong.

He lifted his head from his hands and clasped his palms together. "Dear God," he spoke out loud, "let me live with myself again and put this accursed episode behind me. My love for the South and that war blinded me. I aided and abetted the most hated murderer on earth, convinced the cause was just. But now, I need your guidance to get through each day for the rest of my life as your servant. Please have mercy on Mr. Lincoln's soul, bless and keep him." He took a ragged breath and released a sob. "And please, Father...forgive John Wilkes Booth, for he did not know what he was doing."

Wondering how his mother was handling all this, he jotted off a quick note to her, promising he'd be home soon.

John approached the telegraph office in the hotel's main hall to find out if Booth was in New York. He picked up a blank and wrote "John Wilkes Booth," giving the number of the house. He paused as gut instinct guided him, tore up the paper, and wrote "J.W.B." with directions, remembering that during his entire association with Booth, they rarely wrote or telegraphed under their real names, but always in a manner that no one could understand but them.

He then telegraphed:

J.W.B. in New York:
   If you are in New York, telegraph me.

John Harrison, Elmira, N.Y.

The operator read it over and said, "Is it J.W.B."

John nodded. "Yes." But he began to tremble. Of course they wanted the whole name. He extended his arm to reach for the message and rip it up, when the door opened and someone said, "Yes, there are three or four brothers of them, John, Junius, Brutus, Edwin, and J. Wilkes Booth."

That confirmed his worst suspicions beyond any doubt. *My God, what have I done?* Regaining his senses, he made a lunge for the dispatch, but the operator slapped his hand over it. "We must file all telegrams."

Knowing it was too late to try to rip it up, for that would raise a red flat right over his head. He turned and walked off. *So be it.* He was powerless to control his fate any longer.

As he headed down the street, head down, flags fluttered at half mast and churchbells tolled their mournful chimes. He assured himself he'd be safe for the time being...if he left town.

On Monday, he bought some New York newspapers. As he sat on a bench skimming the pages, an item snagged his eye. If the news of Lincoln's assassination and his realization who committed it hit him like a sledgehammer, this nearly felled him like a hail of gunfire:

"The assassin of Secretary Seward is said to be John H. Surratt, a notorious secessionist of Southern Maryland. His name, with that of J. Wilkes Booth, will forever lead the infamous roll of assassins."

He could scarcely believe what he saw. He stared at his name, the letters growing as large as mountains and then dwindling away to nothing. *So much for my former connection with him.*

Trying to calm his jittery nerves, he bought himself a train ticket.

John jumped down from his rail car on the passenger platform at the Lake Street depot and entered a very wary St. Albans, Vermont. The previous fall, First Lieutenant Bennett Young leading twenty cavalrymen had come in from Canada and taken over the town. With his gun drawn, Young had dramatically mounted the steps of a downtown hotel and proclaimed: "This city is now in the possession of the Confederate States of America!"

The raiders herded residents into the main square and proceeded to rob the three local banks, making off with over $200,000. As they left, they set fire to every building in their path. Before residents could organize a pursuit, the marauders were well on their way back to the Canadian border.

The Vermont state government enticed the Lincoln administration to demand immediate extradition of these alleged thieves. In defense of these men, Nettie Slater brought official documents that allowed their attorneys to prove one point: the raid was no mere robbery, but an organized campaign of the Confederate Secret Service.

Because the government did nothing to return the bank robbers to Vermont justice, local citizens kept a sharp weather-eye out for strangers. So, of course, John knew he'd attract immediate and unwanted attention as he exited the train. There, he met another nonresident: a stout man of complexion so ruddy it looked like theater make-up, adorned with dense, dark whiskers. But they expressed instant recognition of each other.

John extended his hand. "As I live and breathe! So good of you to meet me—"

"Smith, sir, John Smith," the bearded man interrupted in a unnaturally high tenor voice, shaking hands vigorously. "And you are—"

"H-H-Harrison, John Harrison of Montreal," John stammered to Nettie Slater in man's garb, with a pillow gut and bewiskered face and...flattened breasts! A long-lost warmth stirred him deep inside. Oh, to see her again, even looking like this!

"Ah, yes, Mr. Harrison," Nettie went on. "The Canadian General Lee, not the Virginia Lee who surrendered to General Grant on Palm Sunday, sent me to bring you and any of your men back to Montreal."

"I am alone, presently. My former companion seemingly has gone another way. Is there someplace we can rest?" He dropped his valise on the ground and stretched his weary arms. "I am dog tired in every way."

"I know how you feel. Perhaps we could retire to the American House for some refreshment and a light breakfast." Her perfect white teeth peeked out from the whiskers as she smiled. They walked out of the depot into town.

~

As the two strangers passed the station saloon, William Conger stood in the doorway of his not-yet-open tavern. His eyes followed them and his jaw dropped. "Great Caesar's ghost!"

He leapt inside his barroom and shuffled through the morning's *Burlington Times*.

The more pages he turned, the faster he went, ripping some in his haste. At last! A description of President Lincoln's murderer, John Wilkes Booth. The actor. A well-dressed fop. Like the tall man who just passed by. *Could that be Booth?* A co-conspirator, perhaps? Confederate spies! Yes! He'd bet his life on it. He peeked back out into the street, but they were nowhere to be seen.

~

John and his affable companion sat in the small crowded eating room at the American House. His intense feelings for her still consumed him—they'd never waned, even after all this. He longed to tear that disguise off her. "Nettie, I..."

"No, not here!" Nettie glared at him. "Just keep up the charade, lest someone catch on," she intoned softly. "I want to assure you, Mr. Harrison," she spoke again louder and rougher, "that your namesake has been very busy in upstate New York, publicly spreading your name and presence around in Elmira and Canandaigua."

"Then everything is working according to plan?" John's tone lilted for the first time in how long, he couldn't remember.

"So far, Mr. Harrison, so far. I see you have the requisite goatee and moustache to match your double." She studied his features. He squirmed under her scrutiny, remembering how fast he'd fallen head over heels for her and never got over her.

"Well, mine is a little sparse." He ran a hand over his chin. "I never did need to shave much."

"He did a good job with your name at the hotels, too." Her lips curved in a slice of a smile.

"Amazing how a body can forge another's signature so easily." John scowled, not so happy about this expert forger faking *his* name.

"Segar?" she asked. "Or maybe you would like another coffee?"

"No, I'm fine." *Will she whip out a segar and start smoking?* He wouldn't put any gesture past her, since she'd gone to this extreme.

Nettie checked her pocket watch. "We better get back to the depot—don't want to miss our train." As they ambled back to the Lake Street depot, he wished they could've held hands.

~

Again, barkeeper Conger saw them. He closed and locked the tavern door. He would not let these potential assassins get away again. He needed a police officer, but as usual, none was available.

Conger watched the two suspects sit on a bench at the station. Then he hurried toward the American House, where he met banker Albert Sowles and his brother Edward, an attorney. "I need to show you somebody! Come quick!"

As a victim of the Rebel bank heist last fall, Sowles was more than ready to help. He eyed the tall suspect from his vantage point. "No dice." He shook his head. "That's not John Wilkes Booth. The light haired man is too tall and the dark man too uncouth." His brother agreed. "We've been looking at them while they ate, and neither looks like Booth."

"Let's go down and look again." Conger headed for the door. "C'mon. The dark haired one walks funny."

"What do you mean, *funny?*" Ed Sowles cocked a brow.

"I can't put my finger on it." He shrugged. "Just different, I tell you."

All three men returned to the station platform. But they failed to get a good enough look. They kept changing positions as they talked.

~

John noticed the three citizens' interest in him and Nettie.

"Don't look now, but those three men are staring at us," he whispered out the side of his mouth, keeping his eyes averted. "They might be Federal agents. Let's move around a bit to keep them engaged. Check them out. One looks like a bartender—got an apron on under his coat."

Nettie glanced their way. "They have to be local men. They are curious, but still too unsure to move."

"Well, the joke's on them." John turned to face the tracks. "Here comes our train." A distant whistle floated through the air. The train clattered down the tracks and screeched into the depot. They climbed aboard and left the curious residents of St. Albans behind, no wiser than when they'd first shown up.

~

"By gosh, that's a woman!" Conger yelled to his companions. But the train had already pulled out, leaving Conger and the Sowles brothers standing on the platform staring dumbly at one another.

CHAPTER 16

AFTER A TWENTY-FOUR MILE JAUNT, John and Nettie, still disguised, arrived at Rouse's Point. John wanted to get down but she clutched his arm. "No. Stay on the train. If you get off, we'll only attract more curious onlookers and even possibly detectives. It's essential that we keep moving ahead of them. We'll be safely across the border almost as soon as we start."

As John knew from previous trips, the train was divided into two sections at Rouse's Point, one going across New York, the other headed for Montreal. He and Nettie arrived at the capital of British colonial government and debarked for the short trip to the St. Lawrence Hotel, the Canadian locus of Confederate Secret Service activity. He checked in as "Charley Armstrong."

General Edwin Lee paid John $40 for expenses and $100 for services rendered. "Make yourself scarce posthaste," he warned.

When teatime came, one of John's Confederate contacts went down alone. "I'm leery of you showing yourself even in this bastion of Confederate loyalty," Nettie told John.

~

"Where is your handsome friend?" one lady inquired at the tea table. "The tall one. You should have brought him to tea."

"Well, ma'am, you know how it is with Americans. They seldom appreciate the finer things in life. He and his companion dislike tea."

"Tell me, is it true that you have the assassin Booth ensconced upstairs?" joked another tea drinker.

"Oh, one never knows about such things," John's benefactor gave a coy reply. Their goodhearted laugh hung in the air.

~

"Harrison, you need to get out of here at once," the Rebel contact said when he came up from tea. "Even the attempts at humor are getting too close to the truth. After dark, I'll take you to Porterfield's."

"Who's that?" The suspicion in John's tone matched his apprehension.

"Porterfield is from Tennessee and came up here early in the war to help the Confederate Secret Service. He's reliable and succors agents who need a secure resting place outside the St. Lawrence Hotel."

As John and Nettie ambled over to Porterfield's, John happened to see his old friend Lou down the street. "Now what in Sam Hill is *he* doing here?" John wondered out loud. Then it dawned on him. *Looking for me, what else?* He stood talking with a man John did not know, but who looked very much like a policeman or some kind of Federal agent or spy—tough, burly, uncompromising, backed by authority.

"Don't ask questions!" John grabbed Nettie's elbow. "In here!"

John and Nettie ducked into a store doorway and watched the men stroll on toward the St. Lawrence Hotel. "Whew, that was close!" he muttered.

"Wasn't that Lou Weichmann from Washington?" Nettie turned to John. "That man with him looked like a detective."

"It's him, all right." *Damn that Lou*, John swore under his breath. "Now I know he can't be trusted. He'd sell his mother up the river for a few greenbacks."

"If we Confederates know of Porterfield's," Nettie persisted, "I wouldn't be surprised if the United States government does, too!"

"You're right," John agreed, fighting a tingle of fear. "Let's get outta here."

They went back to Porterfield and told him what had happened. "The same two men had already been by to visit me and offered me $20,000 if he would give you up, John," Porterfield said. "So I guess Harrison is an alias," he added. "But don't worry." He sported a cocky grin. "I have contacts who can get you out of here tomorrow. We have to hurry, as those men may come back."

"Give us an hour to get out and then notify them I am here and collect the reward," John suggested. "Leave Nettie out of it."

Porterfield passed John and Nettie on to other Confederate operatives that night. Two coaches headed in opposite directions to confuse anyone watching. John then met another agent who took him down to the St. Lawrence River and rowed him across in a canoe. A woman met them on the opposite shore and led John to the home of Joseph du Tilly, a local woodcutter and hunter. Du Tilly then took John to his brother-in-law, Reverend Father Charles Boucher, who would keep John hidden, incommunicado with the rest of the world for the next three months, before hastening him out of Canada to Europe.

He never saw Nettie Slater again. For that matter, neither did anyone else. She vanished from the face of the earth.

John got over his lovesickness. But he never forgot her. To reassure himself, he stated out loud, "We'll meet again—in the next world."

CHAPTER 17

August 7, 1865

"Hey, Charley."

Brigadier General Edwin Gray Lee extended his hand to the young man at the table in front of him in the posh dining room of the Riverton Hotel in Quebec Province, British Canada. Newspapers across Canada heralded the arrival of the American Lieutenant General U. S. Grant, Union victor of the War of Rebellion, "one of the most remarkable men in North America," in Montreal on a state visit.

The youth stood, clasped Lee's hand, and shook it earnestly. He was six feet three inches in height, with chestnut hair and a non-matching moustache, set off by a pair of wire-rim spectacles. The hair was dyed and the moustache a mite ragged. The eyeglasses were fake. Had anyone seen the man with his natural sandy hair and usual goatee or Napoleon whiskers under his chin, the form of John H. Surratt Jr., fugitive from Yankee justice with a $25,000 price on his head, he would have been easily recognizable.

Lee turned to the man accompanying John, still

using his *nom de guerre* of Charley Armstrong, and greeted him, "Mr. Bouthillier, good job. You have got our man here in safety."

"Zank you, mon gènèral," Bouthillier thanked him in French-accented English.

"Sir," John addressed General Lee, his tone mournful, "they hanged my mother with Atzerodt, Powell, and Herold. Those sons of bitches hanged my mother like a common criminal. No one even told me about it until it was too late. I swear, I would have gone to Washington City had I but known of it in time." His voice wavered with grief as the shock of that horrifying news revisited him.

"Easy, Charley." General Lee placed his hand on John's shoulder. "There was nothing anyone could have done. They would have hanged you both, if you had come in. We knew that you would have surrendered had you known. We intentionally kept you in ignorance of the situation to save your life."

"Father Boucher's was so far from everything and so isolated. I knew nothing until it was too late. I now appear as an abject coward to the world." John cringed with shame, unable to hold his head up in public.

"Non, non, monsieur," Bouthillier assured him. "Ze world onerstand you position. Yankees appear coward."

"And now I have to run and prove my courage?" John hung his head in despair.

"No, Charley," General Lee said. "You are running, as you put it, because of an unfortunate occurrence."

"The cleaning woman?" John asked.

"Yes." General Lee nodded. "The cleaning

woman at Father Boucher's in St. Liboire. When her natural curiosity, plus the rumors circulating amongst the locals that someone important was hiding there—you know, the various hunting trips by your friends, my purchase of a rifle for your use, and so on—got the best of her and she peeked through the hole in the wall between your place of hiding and the rest of the house, it was all over."

John swore to his Lord under his breath.

"She was so scared when you got up off the sofa and went at her that she ran screaming into the street. Such wild stories as would emanate from such an incident would soon bring the curious to see the 'Specter of St. Liboire.' And the curious would one day be the United States's detectives, seeking your arrest and extradition."

"Now what?" John dreaded the answer, but needed to know.

"It is not yet time for you to be tried. Too much chance that it will still be a military commission, not a civil panel with a jury. There is a case proceeding through the Yankee court system out of Indiana involving the unconstitutionality of military trials during time of war in jurisdictions that have the civil courts still operating. When that case is settled—the defendant is one Lamdin Milligan, I believe—hopefully on behalf of Mr. Milligan, who was sentenced to death for aiding the Confederacy behind Union battle lines, then you may be assured of a fair trial should you be arrested. Until then, the remnants of the Confederate government, with the active cooperation of the Holy Roman Catholic Church, will conceal you."

"Where am I to be stored, if I may ask?" Visions

of the sweltering, stinking jail cell where his mother spent her final days tormented him.

"Certainly. Mr Bouthillier will take you to the Bishop's Palace in Quebec City. You remember father Lapierre of Montreal? His father has a shoe and boot shop behind the Bishop's Palace in Quebec City. You will be concealed there in a back room in the second story of his shop, in the family's living quarters. It should be quite comfortable."

Within a month, John, a.k.a. Charley Armstrong, revealed himself again. Lonely from being shut off from the world, he befriended a lady he'd met at the home of John Lovell, a Confederate sympathizer. Lovell had been housing General Lee in Montreal, and John had been allowed to visit from his Quebec isolation. Lee warned the lady off. But once again, there was an unwanted witness to the presence of Charley Armstrong.

Realizing that John would not agree to stay in isolation any longer, Lee and Father Lapierre went to work and secured him passage on the steamer *Peruvian* for Europe. On September 15, Father Lapierre, in civilian clothes, escorted John to a connecting steamship that deposited them on the *Peruvian* in Quebec City the next day. Father Lapierre placed John in the office of the ship's surgeon, Dr. Lewis McMillan, by prior arrangement. McMillan knew John only as "Mr. McCarty."

The *Peruvian* left port about mid-morning. John, a.k.a. McCarty, wandered the deck, discreetly observing his fellow passengers. He accosted Dr. McMillan after dinner. "Say, Doctor, do you know that man over there?"

"Not personally, no," the doctor replied. "He's just another passenger, like yourself."

"Oh, no. I suspect he's an American detective. A detective after me." John forced a casual tone.

"Indeed? I doubt that. Why should an American detective be after you, anyway?"

"I have done more things than you could possibly be aware of. If you knew all that I have done in an effort to save the South, it would make you stare wide-eyed, I assure you." John didn't know why he was revealing all this to a stranger—he reckoned it was because he knew he had nothing more to lose.

The following day, John arrived in Liverpool. Dr. McMillan reported John's cryptic revelation to the American vice consul, Henry Wilding, who informed him the U.S. government was uninterested in Mr. McCarty at that time. Later, an angry congressional committee would lay all blame for the lack of pursuit at the feet of its arch nemesis during Reconstruction, President Andrew Johnson.

Meanwhile, John was ensconced in a small room at the Oratory of the Holy Cross in Liverpool. His contact there, Father Charles Jolivet, gave John money for a journey to Vatican City. Although he was first refused admittance into the Papal States as an indigent, John had letters of introduction from Liverpool that let him receive fifty francs to change his economic status and gain admission and travel to Rome.

John soon enrolled in the Papal Guards, under the moniker of Giovanni Watson.

John's refuge was soon revealed when, by sheer chance, Henri Beaumont de Ste. Marie, an acquaintance of his and Lou's, recognized him. Ste. Marie went to Rufus King, the U.S. minister to the Papal States, with his identification of John. "I believe he's protected by the Clergy," Ste. Marie alleged, "and that the murder is a result of a deep laid plot not only against the life of President Lincoln, but against the life of the Republic, as we are aware that the priesthood and Royalty are and always have been opposed to liberty."

King forwarded Ste. Marie's statement to Washington, D.C. As he awaited approval to go ahead, King talked to the Vatican's secretary of state, Giacomo Cardinal Antonelli, about the possibility of extraditing John to the United States.

Although John seemed safe from any American prosecution as the Papal States lacked a treaty of extradition with the United States, the threat of the impending Italian conquest of the Papal States left room for maneuver. King and Antonelli agreed that John could be extradited if the U.S. Navy would stand by to evacuate the Pope and Vatican personnel in case of invasion from the hostile Italian secular state.

John's arrest was soon effected. But in the process of being escorted to American jurisdiction, John broke into a run and vaulted over a wall, falling thirty feet to a small ledge. Piles of refuse broke his fall. As his astonished guards looked on, John escaped, miraculously unhurt, beating the chasers to the Italian border. He managed to avoid further pursuit and stowed away on a ship headed for Egypt.

American authorities missed the ship at Malta, but they intercepted John at Alexandria, Egypt. They arrested him, clapped him in irons, and forcibly shipped him back to Washington to face trial. The testimony was so contradictory in the civilian criminal court, guaranteed John by the favorable ruling in *ex parte* Milligan, that the jury was unable to return a unanimous guilty verdict. The military commission that hanged his mother had needed only a two-thirds majority. The final tally was 8-4 in John's favor. Northerners and foreign-born voted to convict—Southerners to acquit. After talk of a new trial, the Federal authorities gave up. No way would a jury of his peers send John to the gallows.

While alone in an anteroom of the courthouse, a youth of about fifteen approached Louis Weichmann, sat on Lou's knees, placed his arms around Lou's neck and kissed him on the cheek.

"I desire to thank you, sir, for your testimony in behalf of my murdered father."

"Who are you, sonny?" Lou asked, unnerved by this display of affection.

"My name is Tad Lincoln," came his answer.

After his release, John tried the lecture circuit, but found audiences too hostile to make it worthwhile. By then, Northerners were tired of hearing how dumb their counter espionage efforts were, and Southerners already knew Yankee incompetence in all aspects of the war to be legion.

In 1866 he admitted, "Damn the Yankees, they have killed my mother, but I have done the Yankees as much harm as I could."

The End

JOHN SURRATT never succeeded in his most important Civil War labors. There were admittedly some deeds of secrecy and some adventure, but John's story lacked piquancy of classical flirtation and courtship, and he never became a heroic figure in his tales. He related a carefully controlled, innocuous story, designed to save his hide, not reveal the truth. Instead of personifying a folk hero, John unintentionally portrayed himself and his companions as a bunch of bumbling incompetents, who could not abduct an unguarded enemy president on a lonely country road. Worse yet, they could not even *find* Lincoln to capture him in theater or highway. John has been judged the best of Booth's band of misfits. Of course Booth succeeded in carrying out his evil deed. But his ragtag band failed to obey Booth's orders, intentionally or not. George Atzerodt lost his nerve and did not kill Vice President Johnson. Lewis Powell seriously injured Secretary Seward in his house, but the Secretary survived due to the metal brace he wore as a result of his previous carriage accident. David Herold escaped with Booth, but surrendered when Union soldiers surrounded them in a barn at Garrett's Farm in Virginia. The four conspirators were apprehended, tried, and found guilty. Mary Surratt was hanged alongside Herold, Atzerodt, and Powell, her daughter's desperate pleas to President Johnson falling on deaf ears. Booth was shot in the burning barn by Sergeant Boston Corbett, claiming that God had told him to kill the assassin. Booth died the next day, uttering his last words, "Tell Mother I died for my country."

After the war, John Surratt moved with his brother and sister to Baltimore. They lost their property in Washington City and the Maryland countryside to debt collectors. Surrattsville was renamed Clinton to remove the stigma of a name associated with Lincoln's assassination. But the Surratt tavern still stands in the middle of town as a state park.

John longed to be a hero—until circumstances thwarted his "heroic" deed of killing General Grant, resolving his agonizing inner conflict. No more did his dilemma—to kill or not to kill—torment him.

He died of pneumonia on April 21, 1916, aged 72, neither a hero nor a sinner. He never wrote his memoirs or revealed anything more on his Civil War experiences. As the last of the surviving so-called Booth co-conspirators, he missed a great chance to have the final authoritative, unchallenged word on the plots against Lincoln. Even John's former friend and later nemesis, Louis Weichmann, left an account upon his death, A TRUE HISTORY OF THE ASSASSINATION OF ABRAHAM LINCOLN AND OF THE CONSPIRACY OF 1865.

Ultimately, only twenty-four Civil War spy memoirs survive—nineteen by men, five by women, seventeen Union, seven Rebel. That John was not among those who told his complete story actually may make him the perfect secret agent—an accomplished liar. Not a habitual liar, but rather one who practiced deception successfully. Like most secret agents on both sides in America's greatest war, he had one supreme virtue—he kept his mouth shut.

Dear reader,

We hope you enjoyed reading *The One That Got Away*. Please take a moment to leave a review, even if it's a short one. Your opinion is important to us.

Discover more books by Diana Rubino at https://www.nextchapter.pub/authors/diana-rubino

Want to know when one of our books is free or discounted? Join the newsletter at http://eepurl.com/bqqB3H

Best regards,

Diana Rubino and the Next Chapter Team

ABOUT THE AUTHOR

Diana writes about folks through history who shook things up. Her passion for history and travel has taken her to every locale of her books: Medieval and Renaissance England, Egypt, the Mediterranean, colonial Virginia, New England, and New York. Her urban fantasy romance FAKIN' IT won a Top Pick award from Romantic Times. She is a member of the Richard III Society and the Aaron Burr Association. With her husband Chris, she owns CostPro, Inc., a construction cost consulting business. In her spare time, Diana bicycles, golfs, does yoga, plays her piano, devours books, and lives the dream on Cape Cod.

Visit Diana at
www.dianarubino.com, www.DianaRubinoAuthor.blogspot.com,
https://www.facebook.com/DianaRubinoAuthor
and on Twitter *@DianaLRubino*.

The One That Got Away
ISBN: 978-4-82411-266-8
Mass Market

Published by
Next Chapter
1-60-20 Minami-Otsuka
170-0005 Toshima-Ku, Tokyo
+818035793528

7th November 2021